The Hunt for the Haunted Elephant

BOOK THREE

The Hunt for the Haunted Elephant

by Carol Matas & Perry Nodelman

KEY PORTER BOOKS

Library and Archives Canada Cataloguing in Publication

Matas, Carol, 1949–

    The hunt for the haunted elephant / Carol Matas and Perry Nodelman.

(Ghosthunters; bk. 3)
ISBN 978-1-55470-265-7

 I. Nodelman, Perry II. Title. III. Series: Matas, Carol, 1949–
Ghosthunters; bk. 3.

PS8576.A7994H86 2010   jC813'.54   C2009-905170-2

**ONTARIO ARTS COUNCIL
CONSEIL DES ARTS DE L'ONTARIO**

The publisher gratefully acknowledges the support of the Canada Council for the Arts
and the Ontario Arts Council for its publishing program. We acknowledge the support of
the Government of Ontario through the Ontario Media Development Corporation's
Ontario Book Initiative.

We acknowledge the financial support of the Government of Canada through the Book
Publishing Industry Development Program (BPIDP) for our publishing activities.

Key Porter Books Limited
Six Adelaide Street East, Tenth Floor
Toronto, Ontario
Canada M5C 1H6
www.keyporter.com

Text design: Alison Carr
Electronic formatting: Marijke Friesen
Printed and bound in Canada
10 11 12 13 14 5 4 3 2 1

We dedicate this book about a brother and a sister
to our siblings: Susan, John, Allan and Joel.

Prologue

*H*e was frightened.

He didn't know why, but he was.

It couldn't be because of where he was. He was in the same old familiar place, and everything looked like it always did. He gazed about. Right next to him was his special tree, the one with the tree house in the upper branches. The tree was one of many that grew around the edge of a small, grassy circle filled with wild-flowers, some just opening now, for it had been a cold spring. There was a glimpse of blue sky through the canopy of leaves.

Yes, it appeared that all was as it should be. So why, then, did a cold chill keep running up and down his spine?

Perhaps he should go and see Momma. It felt like ages since he had seen her. And thinking about it, that was odd, because shouldn't he be in bed? Hadn't he been very ill? He last remembered her hovering over him, tears streaming down her cheeks, saying, "Don't leave, dearest, don't leave." So what, he wondered, was he doing out here in the glen? He supposed he'd gotten better——but he couldn't remember when, or how.

And besides, why not be here? His secret was here, after all.

Maybe it was time to tell Momma what he had done and take his medicine. She wouldn't be angry with him for long. She never was. He should dig the things up now and return them all. It had been a silly thing to do, but Momma would forgive him.

Yes! He'd do it right now. He turned to the spot under the tree where the treasure was buried, crouched, and pushed his hand into the earth so he could begin to dig.

But that couldn't be! It was impossible! His hand was going right through the earth.

He pulled out his hand, and tried again. The same thing happened. And somewhere, someone was laughing. It was a horrible kind of laugh, one that had no fun in it at all. It was mean and nasty and he could tell it was because of the very strange time he was having with his hand.

He leaped to his feet and gazed frantically around the glen. He couldn't see anything. But the laughter became louder and louder until it seemed to totally envelope him. He began to scream.

"Stop! Please! Please stop!"

And slowly, very slowly it did.

He had to get back to Momma. He ran out of the glen.

And then everything went black.

He was frightened.

He didn't know why, but he was.

It couldn't be because of where he was. He was in the same old familiar place . . .

CHAPTER ONE
The Hunt Is On!

Well, thought Adam, the world as they knew it might be about to end—but at least they wouldn't have to endure the end at minus ten degrees, which was what the temperature had been when they left home. As the plane began to descend, Adam could see green, green grass below, not piles of dirty snow. And the trees were in leaf, so it probably wasn't even cold!

Spring break! And here they were in England! "What are you grinning like an idiot about?" Molly grumbled from the seat beside him.

"I'm just glad we're here in one piece," he told her. "And that we aren't at home freezing to death. And plus, I feel better now that we're doing something and going to Toot Baldon."

Toot Baldon. It was a funny name for a village, you had to admit. There were so many good jokes you could make. It made him grin every time he thought about it. In fact, he wanted to say it again.

"Toot Baldon," he said.

Molly made a sort of snorting sound. Adam knew that meant she couldn't argue with anything he had just said, and also that she loved the name, too. Neither of them could resist saying it as many times as possible.

"I agree," said Dad, who was sitting beside Adam. "At least we're doing something. And it would be a shame if the Barnett family was somehow the cause of the end of the world as we know it."

Adam knew that his dad was referring to a song Adam had been forced to listen to over and over again while Dad did the housework. Sure enough, his mom began to sing the refrain: "It's the end of the w—."

Mercifully, the wheels touched down and the sound of the airplane braking drowned out Mom's singing. As they taxied down the runway to the gate, Adam couldn't help but flash back to the events that had brought them here.

First there was his grandfather turning up at the lake last summer—but not alive. No, as a ghost! And then another ghost, Lucinda, turning up too, in order to kill Adam and Molly's dad. They had stopped Lucinda, thanks to Granddad and Reggie, the nurse who had seemingly appeared out of nowhere. For a long time they had thought that Reggie was a ghost as well, until the family had met his twin brother Lennie in

Palm Springs and realized that Reggie and Lennie were real and were connected to the Barnetts because of a ridiculous old elephant. An elephant, of all things! An elephant with two gems in its eyes, and a curse. The gems had been separated and now they needed to be reunited because. . . . Oh no. Mom was singing again.

"It's the end of the trip as we know it," she sang, and Dad joined right in.

Adam was glad to be on the ground. He would have felt bad if Lucinda had decided to take down an entire plane full of innocent passengers just to get rid of his family. But thankfully, the flight had gone smoothly. Not that Lucinda would have hesitated to crash the plane. After all, she had killed Granddad, and *his* father, and *his* father—and Adam knew that if they didn't stop her that he himself was definitely on her death list. It had all started as revenge—Lucinda had been dismissed for stealing one of the gems from that elephant when she'd been employed by Adam's great-great-great grandfather generations ago—but now it was something else. Adam shivered. Now, he thought, she was enjoying herself. And it wasn't only his family at risk anymore. Lucinda seemed to want to destroy everything.

Adam got up as the seat belt sign clicked off and pulled his knapsack down from the overhead bin. He followed his family in the slow shuffle off the plane and into the terminal. After walking for what seemed like fifteen or twenty miles down a series of long corridors, they passed under a sign that read "United Kingdom Border" and entered a huge room full of people standing in the line for immigration.

Mom began singing again. "It's not quite the end of the trip as we know it."

Lame. The words didn't even fit the tune.

Granddad suddenly popped up beside Adam. "We'd better start making some plans. We can begin with a search through the cottage for that elephant, and then—"

"But Dad," said Adam's father to his own father, "it isn't likely that—"

"Funny thing about that elephant," Molly interrupted. "I mean, all the times we visited Gram over the years, and yet I don't remember ever seeing anything like that."

"Me, either," said her dad, "and I grew up in the place."

"I can't say I remember an elephant either," said Granddad. "But the cottage was always filled with so many, many things, it was hard to keep track of them all. The family lived there for generations, after all, and we Barnetts never did like to throw anything away."

That's certainly true, Adam thought. One of the reasons he used to love visiting his grandma was all the stuff she had, on shelves and on top of little tables and filling up every drawer and closet in the place. It was like some strange museum—you never knew what you'd find next.

"I think I remember an elephant," said Mom. "In the little room upstairs, on top of one of the dressers. There were a bunch of animals there, remember?"

"Maybe," said Dad. "Who ever paid any attention to all that junk?"

"I did," said Mom. "There was a crystal giraffe, and a china cat with flowers painted on it, and some silver poodles—and, I think, an elephant."

"An ivory one with no eyes?" said Granddad. "Surely I'd remember that, because—"

"Your passports please." They'd reached the front of the line, and were all standing in a group in front of a high counter, behind which an immigration officer sat. Dad handed over the passports.

"Hmmph," grunted the officer as she looked through them and stamped them one by one.

"And you, sir?" She turned toward Granddad. "May I see your passport?"

Oh no! thought Adam. She can see him! It seemed that some people could see Granddad and some couldn't, and they still hadn't figured out why that was. But it was very bad that this particular person could see him; ghosts don't have passports, do they? What were they going to do now?

Before Adam could think of anything, Granddad solved the problem in his own way.

He disappeared.

For a moment the immigration officer just stared at the place where Granddad had been standing.

"But," she finally said. "He was . . . and then . . . but he couldn't . . ."

Suddenly they were surrounded by immigration officers—at least ten of them, and some even wore holsters with guns in them. The woman behind the counter must have hit an alarm.

"A man with a huge mop of red hair and a loud shirt! He stood right there. And then he was gone."

"I don't see anybody like that," said one of the officers as they all gazed around in every direction. "Which way did he go?"

"No way," the woman said. "He just—well, he just suddenly wasn't there anymore. These people were talking to him, and then . . ."

One of the officers turned to Dad. "Do you know who she means, sir? Who were you talking to?"

"Me?" said Dad. "Talking?"

"Yes, Tim," said Mom. "You were talking to me, remember?"

"Ah, yes. Of course. To you."

"But . . ." The original officer was looking even more confused. "But I'm sure—"

"It's must be very stressful working here, dear," said Mom in a comforting voice. "Perhaps a cup of tea and a bit of rest would help?"

"Check the monitor!" the woman demanded, regaining her composure. "I know what I saw!"

Adam held his breath as another officer played back the feed. The man shook his head. "Nothing," he said. "Only one man with red hair. Look for yourself."

The woman looked. She shook her head in disbelief as another officer grabbed her by the arm. "Come with me, Elsie. And you lot may pass through," he added as he gathered up their passports and handed them to Dad. "Welcome to the United Kingdom."

Adam breathed a huge sigh of relief as the other immigration officers escorted poor Elsie away, and the Barnett family hurried out of the immigration hall. They moved through more lines, picked up their baggage and the car Dad had rented, and left the airport as quickly as they could.

The car could only buckle up four, but since Granddad was a ghost he didn't need a seat belt. He sat, or rather hovered, in between his two grandchildren in the back seat.

"I'm glad that's over," said Adam, as his dad drove out onto the highway.

"Me, too," said Granddad. "I do apologize for all the fuss. It happened so fast, and I just couldn't think of anything else to do except go away as quickly as possible."

"It's okay, Dad," said Adam's dad. "It was our fault, too—we should have warned you about being visible as soon as we got off the plane."

"I'll have to be more careful," said Granddad.

"We'll all have to be more careful," said Mom.

"And that includes you, Timmie," Granddad added. "Make sure you pay careful attention to your driving. You aren't used to driving on the right side of the road."

"Don't you mean the left side?"

"Yes, that's right," said Granddad, "because the right side would be wrong."

The family had made this trip before, of course, when Gram was alive and they had all come to visit her, and once more after she died when Mom and Dad had started to clean the place out. But they hadn't quite got around to finishing the cleanout yet, and the cottage still hadn't been sold. That was a lucky thing. According to Dad, end of the world or no, England was so expensive these days that without a free place to stay they never could have afforded the trip—or pay for Reggie to come, too, once he finished up some work for Mom at the hospital.

Just then the car wavered over onto the other side of the road. Granddad shrieked "Left! Left!" and Dad swerved back again.

"Sorry," said Dad. "I lost my concentration for a minute. I was thinking about all we have to do."

"Oh," said Molly sarcastically, "you mean like finding a jewel in a pendant that could be anywhere in the whole of England or even the world? And like finding the elephant it belongs in that also could be anywhere, and reuniting the jewel in the pendant and the jewel from Reggie's ring and getting them back into the elephant before Lucinda kills us? Never mind also stopping all the ghosts that are hanging around from realizing that they can come back to Earth in their real bodies and squeeze the rest of us out? Like that?"

Adam just rolled his eyes. Molly was grumpy because she hadn't slept on the plane and she was always a bear when she didn't sleep.

"If anyone can do it, the four of you can," said Granddad. "Here Timmie, turn here," he added.

They had arrived.

CHAPTER TWO

Home, Sweet Haunt

They were in Toot Baldon, a tiny village just outside of Oxford, where Barnetts had lived for so many generations. The house was the first on the small, main street—a two-storey building with a modern kitchen and bathroom and a lovely, big fireplace and a staircase to the second floor that Adam remembered as steep and narrow, sort of like something out of a horror movie. Parts of the building dated all the way back to the 1500s, and other parts were quite new.

Molly's dad unlocked the front door and they all went in.

"Ah," Granddad said, looking around the room. "Home at last. It feels very strange to be back here. And without my dear Dora."

"I feel the same way," Dad said.

So did Adam. Without Gram buzzing around and

asking millions of questions and steeping tea and trying to make them all comfortable, it seemed like a
completely different place.

In fact, he realized, it looked like a completely different place. Where was everything?

"Where is everything?" Molly echoed his thoughts
as she dragged her overstuffed suitcase into the room
and plopped her purse down on the table. The house
looked so empty. All of Gram's pictures and knick-
knacks were gone, and so was a lot of the furniture.
There was just one picture hanging in the front room,
a crayon drawing of Adam and Molly that Adam had
made and sent to Gram when he was really young.
Gram loved the picture and had it framed.

"Remember," Dad said, "after we had my dad's papers and his desk sent back home, I hired an auction
company to come and take whatever they thought they
might be able to get rid of and try to sell it. I didn't
think they'd manage to get rid of so much though! It all
seemed so old and outdated."

"I see they didn't take Adam's silly picture," said
Molly as she gazed around the room.

"They obviously know nothing about art," Adam
told her. She was just jealous because Gram had never
framed one of her pictures.

"Malinger or Markinger or something like that,"
said Mom. "I remember getting a cheque from that
company."

"Yes," said Dad. "They never did send me the list they promised. Maybe it's somewhere here in the house."

"So maybe they took the elephant," said Molly. "And maybe not?"

"I can always call the auction house and get another copy of the list," said Dad.

"Or," said Adam, "maybe we'll find it while we're looking for the elephant."

"Adam is right," said Granddad. "There can't be any harm in looking."

"While you do that," said Mom. "I'll drive in to Oxford and get some food. The rest of you can unpack and start looking."

There's no time to lose, that's for sure, thought Molly. She went straight up the narrow staircase and into what had been Gram's room. The bed was still there and a small chest of drawers, but otherwise it was bare of everything. Adam was right behind her. They pulled out the drawers. Empty.

They went into the room that had been their dad's when he was young, the one they always stayed in when they visited, and found the same thing. Two beds, an empty toy box with the paint worn away, an empty chest of drawers with one leg missing and propped up by a piece of wood—and nothing else. So then they raced downstairs, where they found their dad going through the hutch in the dining room. When he looked up at them they knew what he had found. Nothing.

The three of them went into the kitchen together and peered into every drawer, and then into the living room/dining room, where Gram's old couch still sat, covered in what Molly had always thought was a pretty white-and-blue chintz that disguised the strange lumps that were so painful to sit on. There was also an old pine table with plenty of water marks and stains, and three rickety chairs. Otherwise the house was empty.

Molly sighed. Still, she figured she might as well carry her stuff upstairs to the bedroom and get settled in—or as settled in as she could with so little furniture. She picked her purse up off the table.

"What's that?" said Adam.

"What's what?"

He pointed to the table. "That envelope your purse was sitting on."

Molly looked down. An envelope—a big brown one.

"Messinger and Messinger," she real aloud. "Auction house."

"It's the list!" said Adam. "It must be. It was under your purse the whole time!" He reached over, grabbed the envelope, and tore it open.

"Receipt," he read. "One leather chair, slightly worn. One sterling silver duckling wearing a baby blue woolen scarf and beanie."

And so on. "And there's a picture of each of them, too! It is the list!" He rifled through the stack of papers.

"It's really long."

"Well," said Dad, "there was a lot of old stuff here. You wouldn't believe the size of the cheque they sent me."

"Let's see, Adam," said Molly, snatching the papers back from him. "Is there a sapphire pendant or an antique Indian elephant listed?"

"I wouldn't expect to find the sapphire pendant there, Molly," said Granddad, hovering half-visibly behind her as he tried to read the list over her shoulder. "It was lost years and years ago, remember? Long before I was born. And I certainly don't remember it myself."

"Here it is!" Molly said, stabbing her finger on one of the pages. "One carved elephant, antique ivory, depicted with its trunk auspiciously raised, eye sockets blank, provenance unknown." She held the paper up so everyone could see the photograph.

"That's it?" asked Adam. The photograph, small and printed on an ordinary sheet of white paper along with pictures of a bunch of other things, was kind of fuzzy, but it was clear enough to show that the elephant was small and rather plain.

"Hold it up toward me, Molly," said Granddad. She did. "Hmm," he said. "It looks like something you'd buy from a souvenir store. I don't recognize it. In fact, I'm pretty positive that I've never seen it before."

"But the auction people did find it in the house,"

said Dad. "Maybe it was hidden away up in the attic or somewhere."

"And hey," said Adam, "maybe Gram found it one time when she was cleaning, and brought it down and cleaned it up. You know how she loved fiddling around with all her things, moving them into different arrangements and all."

"Yes," said Dad, "she did, didn't she?"

"Really?" said Granddad. "I don't remember her doing that. I guess she was too busy for it when you were a young lad, Timmie, and getting into scrapes all the time. Oh, dear. I missed so, so much!"

Adam didn't know what to say to stop his granddad from being so unhappy. Luckily Molly, who was still reading the list, interrupted.

"There's no sapphire pendant here," she said.

"Rats," said Dad.

Adam was impressed. Compared to the language his dad usually used when upset, "rats" was mild. Perhaps being in England and in his childhood home, he was reverting to behaviour Gram would approve of.

"At least we know that the auction people didn't find it here," said Granddad. "And they must have done a pretty thorough search. And we also know the elephant was here, and we know that the auction house put it on sale. So at least we have somewhere to start."

Granddad was right, thought Adam. They needed to stay calm and keep plugging away at their search.

There was no use panicking until they'd tried everything and failed. Still, he was worried, very worried. It could be a long search, and it could end up being fruitless anyway. And would Lucinda hunt them down before they could find it? He was starting to feel a bit dizzy—whether from fear or the long trip, he wasn't sure.

He needed some fresh air. As Dad, Molly, and Granddad discussed what to do next, he went outside and took a few deep breaths. He immediately felt much, much better. He decided to do a little exploring, to see if things were any different than the last time he had been here in Toot Baldon, a few years ago. He headed around to the back of the house. There were farmers' fields behind the garden, sometimes with flocks of sheep, and looking at them always made him feel calmer. And there, just behind Gram's old barn, was the small grove of trees Adam had always loved— it was the best place for thinking and dreaming and imagining anywhere in the entire world.

He walked over to it, sat beneath his favourite tree, and gazed up.

Yup. The tree house was still there—a little shabby but still hanging on. Barnett Bonkers, he found himself thinking.

It was Granddad and Dad's secret password for the tree house—the one Granddad had told them about at the lake last summer. The tree house seemed different now that Adam knew about the password. If Adam climbed the tree and said it, would there be a younger version of Dad up there, waiting to let him in?

Nonsense, he thought. Dad was still alive, thank goodness, and in the house right now. Adam didn't need any secret password to find him. So much for Barnett Bonkers.

As the phrase passed through his mind once more, a young boy appeared right in front of him; a boy of about eight with bright red hair.

"Oh, hello," the boy said. "Do you know where my momma is?"

CHAPTER THREE
A Haunted Glade

Adam decided he'd better think for a moment before he replied. Had this boy just appeared out of nowhere, or was it—as Molly would say—Adam's overactive imagination that made him jump to the conclusion that he was seeing a ghost? He did tend to see ghosts everywhere these days, but who could blame him? It was bad enough when Granddad had suddenly shown up behind his desk at the cottage last summer, and then things had gotten worse in Palm Springs, when the Barnetts' lives were filled with ghosts of every sort, from former neighbours and assistants to a walking skeleton. Once you knew about them and could see them, they did seem to be everywhere.

And most of them appeared to be pretty harmless—except for Lucinda, of course, who was just plain deranged. But the others only seemed to want a little attention——someone to listen to their sad tales of woe. They weren't even all that scary, really, once you got used to them. Not anywhere near as creepy as real things like leeches or snakes, or wasps, or bad thunderstorms with lightning that could kill you, or what about all those germs hiding in food? Adam shuddered thinking about the recent hot dog recall. Hot dogs that could kill you. Now that was scary!

He realized he'd been staring at the boy for a very long time and that he'd better do or say something. And hey, maybe it was just a fast-moving real kid this time and not a ghost at all. True, he was dressed a little strangely, in a sort of long robe-like thing, like an old-fashioned nightgown. But it was England, after all. Who knew what the latest fashion statement was?

"Uh, I haven't seen your mom, no," he answered the boy calmly. "Are you lost?"

"Oh no!" exclaimed the boy. "I live just over there" and he pointed toward the house, "in The Oaks, Toot Baldon."

As he said Toot Baldon, the boy smiled a little. Did he think the name was fun to say, too? Adam smiled back, but his heart sank a little too. The boy thought he lived there, in the deserted and almost empty cottage. In Gram's house. He must be a ghost after all.

If he was a ghost, he wasn't a very scary one. He was younger than Adam had thought at first, maybe six or seven years old, and very pale. He looked thin enough for a light breeze to knock him over.

And if he lived in Gram's cottage, he might be a relative. Adam decided to see if he could find out more.

"That's interesting," said Adam, "because I was just there myself, and, well, it seemed deserted. It doesn't look like anyone is living there right now."

"Don't be silly," the boy said, "we all live there, my momma and my poppa and me. And my older brother sometimes when he comes to visit. But what were you doing there?" The boy stared at him for a moment. "Are you my cousin Paul?" he asked.

"No, my name is Adam."

"Because," the boy continued, "Momma tells me that my cousin Paul is quite the joker and she's been promising me for ages that he would come and visit us—here in Toot Baldon—and I'd see how funny he is. And now you're here and you're joking, aren't you? And you do look a bit like all my cousins. We've all got the same hair." At this he pointed to his mop of red hair and then to Adam's.

"Oh," Adam smiled. "I see what you mean. But I'm not Paul. My name is Adam. Adam Barnett."

"Aha!" said the boy. "We must be cousins, then, because my name is John Barnett." And he held out his hand to shake Adam's.

So the boy was a relative! Adam reached up to grasp his hand.

31

Adam's hand went right through John's. Well, that settled it. The boy was a ghost—no question about it.

Unfortunately, however, John didn't seem to realize that he was a ghost. He was staring at his own hand now, and then at Adam's with a perplexed look on his face. Then he reached out and tried shaking Adam's hand again.

The same thing happened. "It . . . it's just like before," John said. "When I tried to dig for the things. Why do I keep going through things? What's wrong with me? What's wrong with you?" His eyes filled up and he began to cry.

It was just a very slow trickle of tears. It was as if the boy was so confused he couldn't even concentrate on having a good cry, thought Adam. "It's okay, John," Adam said. "Really. Well, maybe not really, because, well, it might take some getting used to, but I think I can explain it to you. You see, you're a g—"

It was just then that Molly burst into the grove.

"Ah, Adam," she exclaimed, "there you are!"

John blinked out the second she appeared.

"Reggie called from Heathrow to say that he's arrived in England," she said. "The work he had to do at the hospital took less time than he thought it would. And Mom's back from Tesco's with food—aren't you hungry?"

"I've just been talking to a ghost," said Adam.

"A ghost? Are you sure?" Molly never knew how

much of what Adam said was to be believed. After all, he'd once told her he'd seen a giant water snake right in front of their cabin at the lake. And then there were the little green men lurking in his frozen peas, and that boy in Adam's school, Tyson McMahon or something, who Adam was convinced was a vampire.

"Oh, he's a ghost all right," said Adam very calmly. "No question about it."

"Well," she said, "we have been seeing lots of ghosts lately. But what makes you think—"

"We tried to shake hands."

Molly's eyebrows went up. "Oh. I get it. Your hand went through his?"

"Yup."

"I hate it when that happens," she shuddered, remembering times when she'd leaned over too fast or something and accidentally got mixed up inside one of her granddad's arms. "So who is he? Someone we know?"

Another thought struck her. "It isn't someone Lucinda sent to spy on us, is it? Does she already know we're here? Because if she does we have to—"

"Hold on, Molly," said Adam. "I don't think he's a spy. He's only about six or seven years old. And he doesn't even seem to realize that he's a ghost. He thinks he still lives over there in Gram's house."

"Oh," she said, "poor little thing."

"And he's most likely our cousin. That's what he thinks, anyway, and I bet he's right. Or maybe a great-

great-uncle or something. But he's related to us for sure, because he says his name is John Barnett."

"There are lots of Barnetts who aren't related to us, Adam."

"But they don't think they live in Gram's house in Toot Baldon. And that isn't all: he has bright red hair."

"Sounds like a relative, all right," said Molly, secretly grateful that she hadn't inherited that red hair the way her father and her brother had. It would be way too hard to find outfits to match it. Strawberry blonde was much better.

"I was trying to explain to him about being a ghost, when you showed up," said Adam, "but I don't think it was going very well. He seems so clueless. And it can't be much fun when someone tells you you're dead. Remember the way Granddad acted when he found out?"

Molly did remember. It almost killed him. Again.

"What I'd like to know," said Adam, "is why we're suddenly seeing John here? I mean, we've never seen him here before, right? And I never heard Gram or Dad mention seeing the ghost of a boy here either. It must have something to do with Lucinda and all the rest of it. It has to. But what?"

"Well, we never used to see any ghosts," Molly reminded him.

"If we could figure out which relative he is—if we knew when he was alive—maybe that would give us a hint," Adam said, continuing his train of thought. "But the Barnetts have lived in this cottage for an awfully long time. How can we figure out when John was here?"

"There's probably an answer in all those papers that came with Granddad's desk," said Molly. "Too bad they're all back home."

"Yes, but Granddad might know. We could ask him if he knows of any Barnetts called John."

"He does know an awful lot about the family history," said Molly. "But if John is a ghost and still only a boy, he must have died when he was awfully young. Would Granddad know about that?"

"There's only one way to find out," said Adam. "Granddad?" he called, "Are you around here somewhere? Because if you are——"

"Were you looking for me?" It was the boy John again. He had suddenly blinked into view and stood in between Adam and Molly. "I thought I heard someone calling."

John was staring now, first at Adam and then at Molly, and then back at Adam. "That's a very strange outfit you're wearing," he said to Adam. Then he turned to Molly. "And yours is even stranger."

Adam couldn't remember what he had on—what with theorizing and inventing and all, he didn't really have much time to think about clothes, which drove his sister crazy, because she had lots of time for it. He looked down to see that it was just his usual: jeans and a T-shirt. They were pretty wrinkled and messy from the plane trip, but nothing special. And Molly had on jeans and a T-shirt, too. Of course, the jeans had a silly orange paisley pattern down the side, and her long brown top was covered with a short orange jacket, also with paisleys. But it was really still just jeans and a T-shirt.

"You look sort of like farm labourers" said John, "but with bright colours and no mud stains and much, much fancier. Is there a fancy dress ball? I like fancy dress balls! Except I have no costume." He looked down at his own clothing. "Oh dear," he said, with a puzzled look on his face. "I really shouldn't be out here in my nightdress. Someone passing by might see me. And Momma will be very displeased. She'll worry about me catching a chill. I'd best go back to the house and get changed. Please do excuse me."

He turned and walked past Molly toward the house and then, as he reached the edge of the clearing, suddenly blinked out of view again.

Molly looked at Adam and again said, "Poor thing! I wonder why he's dressed in a nightgown."

"Maybe," said Adam, "he died at night, in his bed."

"He probably did," said Molly. "Lots of kids died in the olden days of just about anything. Granddad will probably know if we can only—"

Once more, John was back.

"That's very odd indeed," he said. "I was going home and yet somehow I ended up back here."

Very interesting, thought Adam. Every time we

mention Granddad, John appears. I wonder if that means anything?

"I really would like to go home now," he told Molly. "Can you help me get home?"

Tears burned in Molly's eyes. The poor child had no idea what had happened to him, no idea at all. "Come sit down here with us for a moment," she said gently. "We need to talk to you. It won't take long, and then we'll try to help you get home again."

"All right," he said hesitantly. "But I do need to hurry home and change into my trousers."

"Let's sit here," said Molly. She plopped herself down under the tree and patted the ground.

Still confused, John sat down beside her. Adam sat on his other side.

"I don't mind sitting here," he said, "because it's my favourite tree. It is, you know, my very favourite. My poppa built me that tree house."

"We need to ask you some questions, John," said Molly. "Is that all right?"

John nodded, looking up at her. The trust on his face was heartbreaking. He was totally convinced that she was going to help him.

"Tell me," Molly said, "What's your name? I mean your whole name."

"It's John Barnett. John Maurice Barnett."

"And do you know your mommy and daddy's names?"

"My momma and poppa? Yes, of course I do. My momma is Momma Barnett and my poppa is Poppa."

Well, thought Adam, he *is* very young. Adam himself probably wouldn't have known his parents' first names when he was that age.

"Of course," Molly continued. "Do you know what year it is now, John?" Maybe if they could give Granddad the year, he could figure out who John was.

"I don't think so," said John. "I know it's October. At least I think it is. Is it?"

"Uh, no," said Molly. "Not really." And she couldn't think of anything else to ask. It was time to tell him. "John," she began, "can you tell me the last thing you remember? Before you came here and found Adam and me, I mean?"

He thought for a while, his brow wrinkled. "I remember being sick," he finally answered. "And Momma was crying. And then—well—here I am. Outside. Again. In my nightie." He paused. "I don't want to give her something else to be upset with me about." He stopped again and thought for a moment, looking very worried. "And that's another thing," he continued. "Something is not quite right with my hands. Look." He tried to dig in the ground. His hand went right through the grass and disappeared. He pulled it out again and stared at it for a moment, and then, suddenly, slammed his fingers into his nose.

"Ouch!" he said. "That hurts! But at least it didn't

go right through. That's one good thing." He held his nose in his hands, looking very unhappy.

"John," Molly said, wishing she could hold his little hand and knowing it was impossible, "I'm afraid— well, I'm afraid you were too sick to get better. I'm afraid you—"

"You died, John," said Adam, desperate to get the whole miserable business over. It was too painful to watch the little boy be so confused. The truth might be awful, but at least he wouldn't be so bewildered anymore.

"You aren't alive anymore," Molly added.

"Don't be silly," he said. "I'm talking to you, aren't I? How could I be talking to you if I weren't alive?"

"It because you . . . you . . ."

"You're a ghost," said Adam.

"That's right," said Molly. "A ghost."

CHAPTER FOUR
A Haunt Who Hurts

For a moment or two John just sat there and stared at them. Then he smiled. "Are you his sister?" he asked Molly, pointing toward Adam.

"Yes," Molly said, "I am. My name is Molly."

"Molly Barnett, correct?"

"Right."

"Barnett—just like him. And Poppa and Momma and me. But you talk funny. Are you from across the pond?"

The pond? thought Molly. Oh yes—that's what people in England called the Atlantic Ocean. "Yes, we are."

"I thought so." He grinned in relief. "Well, that explains it, then! My momma told me that the Barnetts are all jokesters."

"But John," said Molly, "we're not joking."

"We aren't," said Adam. "Really and truly."

"You can't fool me," said John, smiling again. "We Barnetts are all alike. I can't possibly be a ghost, and you know it. You think we English lads aren't clever but we are. So there!"

"Adam! Molly!"

It was their mom calling them to come and eat.

Adam sighed. He was very, very hungry, of course, even though he'd eaten all of the pitiful excuse for a breakfast they'd handed out to him on the plane, and most of Molly's and his Mom's, too. Even the pale yellow sludge they called scrambled eggs. But it was hardly surprising, because he was always hungry.

He might as well give convincing John one more try.

"We probably really are your relatives, John," he said. "But many years later, after you were alive. Maybe more than a whole century later."

"Yes, of course," said John. "You're from the future! And I'm Queen Victoria." He giggled.

"The Queen is Elizabeth now," said Molly, "and Victoria was her great-grandmother or something like that. I don't know, maybe even her great-great-grandmother."

"Like maybe your father was our great-great-grandfather," added Adam thoughtfully. "Or maybe your brother? Did you have any brothers or sisters, John?"

"I have a much older brother," John answered, "but

he doesn't live here anymore. He's married now to my new sister Gwendolyn. His name is Percy."

"Percy," said Adam. "That's my middle name. Interesting."

"It's Granddad's middle name, too, Adam," added Molly. "It's an old family name, remember? Granddad told us it came down from his great-granddad."

"Right," Adam remembered. "His great-granddad was Percy!"

"Molly? Adam?" Mom was shouting from the house again. "The soup is getting cold."

"Coming!" shouted Adam.

"This is silly," said John, standing up and looking very upset. "You pretending I'm dead, I mean."

"We're sorry, John," said Adam, "but—"

"It's like my momma says," added John. "When you take a joke too far it stops being funny. Please stop it, right now."

"But John," Molly began, "we—"

"If you don't stop it, I'll—I'll give you a big hit!" As he said it, he leaned forward and pushed his arms into Adam's belly . . . except his arms went right through Adam, and John fell down to the ground. Well, actually, he fell down *into* the ground, and then slowly rose back up, looking even more upset. He stared at the ground and then at them.

"You're not joking?" he said in a very small voice. "You're telling the truth?"

"I'm afraid so," said Molly, wishing even more that she could take him into her arms and comfort him.

But she couldn't. She could only watch as he stood there, shivering, confused, and pathetic.

"Dead." he said. "A ghost."

Then a look of panic came onto his face.

"I can't be dead," he cried. "I can't, I just can't!"

"It'll be okay, John," said Adam. "I'm sure it'll be okay." It sounded totally lame, but he didn't know what else to say or do. What if someone suddenly told him he was dead? What would he do?

Just what John was doing. "I can't, I can't," John repeated. He turned to Molly. "I did something. Something awful . . . I need to make it better. Oh no!"

John fell to his knees and began pulling at the ground with his fingers. The more he clawed it and the more the dirt remained undisturbed, the more loudly he bawled. "I can't, I can't, I can't!"

"Just tell us," Molly pleaded. "Tell us what it is and we'll help you,"

"No!" He leaped up screaming. "I can't be dead! I can't!"

And then he was gone.

Adam and Molly looked at each other, both shaking their heads.

"That went well," Adam said.

"Just peachy," added Molly. "But now what? Do we wait until he comes back?"

44

"If he does come back. If I were him, I'd want to stay as far away from the two of us as I possibly could."

"I don't know about you," said Molly, "but I'm starving! Let's go eat something that actually looks like and tastes like food. The plane stuff was something else altogether. And while we're eating we can ask Grand-dad about all this. He's the ghost expert, after all."

And that was when they heard it. A loud laugh, high and screeching and horrible.

Molly grasped Adam's arm. "Is that Lucinda?"

"But we just got here," Adam said. "How could she even know we're here?"

"Why not?" said Molly. "She found us back home, right? And she knew when we went to Palm Springs, too. It's like she has a direct line to us or something."

Adam shivered. That was too awful to even think about.

Someone—or something—had produced that laugh. And whether it was Lucinda or not, it was a hor-rible reminder that their time was limited. They needed to find a way to stop her—and other spirits from dis-covering that ghosts could return in their own bodies. And to do that they had to get in touch with the auc-tion house, and then they had to find out if anyone bought the elephant, and then they had to try to get it back. They also had to find the sapphire necklace, which had been lost—or stolen, or maybe even destroyed—for more than a hundred years. They had no idea how much time they had. But it could be hours rather than days, or, at the very least, days rather than weeks!

"Let's get back to the house," Adam said, and he began to head in that direction.

CHAPTER FIVE
Hunting Plans

Mom had put quite a spread out on the dining room table, not only soup but things in jars and sliced meats and vegetables—a whole lot of different kinds of vegetables.

"I just couldn't resist the vegetables," Mom said. "They always look so fresh and tasty here—not like those awful things we get back home this time of the year that come from thousands of miles away and taste like wood."

Adam had to admit it—the tomatoes and cucumbers and pea-pods and celery and carrots did look good. Even the cut up cauliflower looked good, as long as you didn't actually have to eat it. But it was the sliced meat that really interested him, and some cheese would be okay too. He grabbed a piece of bread and slathered it with mustard and began to pile cheese and salami and ham on it, and also something that looked like corned beef, and something else that—

"What this stuff?" he asked, pointing to the strange-looking sliced meat on one of the plates.

"That's headcheese," Mom said. "A traditional British delicacy, although they call it 'brawn' here."

"It looks like meat," he said. "Not cheese." It actually looked like bits of meat floating in something like jello.

"It *is* meat," she said.

"Oh. Good. I like meat." He stuffed a slice into his mouth. It wasn't bad. A little chewy, but not bad at all.

"It's the meat from a cow's head," Mom continued. "Or maybe a pig's head. They take the head and boil it up until the meat falls off, and then they shred the meat and put it back in the water it boiled in and let it cool, and voila! It's headcheese! Or brawn. I haven't had it in years."

Cow head or pig head? Adam choked. He grabbed a napkin, spat it out, and then wadded up the napkin and looked for somewhere to dump the whole mess. No one had made any garbage yet, but he saw that his mom had put some garbage bags on the counter. He opened one and stuffed the wad of—ugh—boiled head parts into it.

"Mom!" he exclaimed, "You could've warned me. I might never eat again!"

"I doubt that, Adam," his mom said calmly.

And, in fact, it did occur to him that a pile of salami and ham would be just the thing to get that awful taste out of his mouth. He grabbed the sandwich he'd been making, added some sliced turkey to it and then took a huge bite, hoping his mom wouldn't come up with some horror story about how they made salami.

Unfortunately, there weren't enough chairs left in the house for everyone to sit on, but Adam didn't care. He wolfed his food down standing, as did Mom, who was eating headcheese and, apparently, enjoying it.

Molly sat on one of the chairs that had been left behind, trying to eat something in the hope that it would take the queasiness away. That laugh had sent quite a chill through her. Still, she did start to feel better after a little soup, some fresh bread slathered with butter and a mound of veggies topped with cheese— normal cheddar, not the weird stuff—all washed down with something called orange squash, which she remembered from the last time they'd been in England.

In between bites, Adam tried to fill his parents in on the ghost they'd met outside. Granddad was particularly interested.

"John Barnett," he mused. "It doesn't ring a bell, I'm afraid. I can't think of one of our ancestors named John."

"But he must have been really young when he died," said Adam. "So he wouldn't have had children or anything."

"Yes," said Granddad. "I suppose he would be just a footnote in the family history. Poor lad."

"And he told us he had an older brother named Percy," said Molly, "That's a family name, right?

"Yes, of course, it's a common family name. And this little boy obviously has a tie to something or some-one here in Toot Baldon, or else he would have moved on long ago. But it doesn't often happen to one so young—being tied like that, I mean. You don't meet many young ones out there on the astral plane. What awful thing could be on the mind of a small child like that, so awful that it holds him here?"

"He seemed worried about something in the ground," said Molly. "Under the tree. Maybe a dead pet that was buried there?"

"Maybe," said Adam. "Or maybe it wasn't really all that awful. Sometimes little kids make a big deal out of little things. Sometimes they don't know any better." Adam was thinking of the time when he was five or six and he'd poured himself a glass of juice then accident-ally dropped the glass and broke it. He'd carefully swept up all the pieces and hid them so his parents wouldn't be mad at him, and then got a terrible stom-ach ache worrying over it and had to be taken to the emergency room. When he finally told his mom and dad about the glass it turned out they didn't even care.

"Maybe," said Granddad. "But this is the first time we've ever seen him. Why now?"

"It really was so sad," Molly chimed in. "Poor little thing didn't even realize he was dead. And," she added ruefully, "he didn't take it all that well when we told him."

"I shall try to find out more about him," said Granddad. "I'll see if I can get him to appear to me. And I really should be making use of all these spirits who keep bothering me all the time. What's the good of having connections on the spiritual plane if you can't make use of them? Perhaps it's time to see if I can locate the Barnett who started the whole thing. You know, Maurice, the one who received the elephant from Fitzie and then took out the jewels and had the ring and the pendant made. That fellow was responsible for a lot of trouble. He might still be hanging around here somewhere, too. I should call him."

"Good plan," said Dad. "And while you're at it we'll drive into Oxford and pay a visit to the auctioneers— see if we can track down the elephant and the pendant."

"They might still have the elephant," Molly said, "and even if someone bought it, the auction house should be able to help us track it down. But the pendant is another matter, isn't it? I mean, we've gone through all the papers and so far there's no sign of where or even when it disappeared. All we know is what we already knew from that diary that Reggie and Lennie's ancestor Fitzie wrote: that it vanished off Maude Barnett's dressing table some time after the emerald ring was stolen."

Molly was feeling quite gloomy again. How were they going to beat Lucinda? Right now it seemed pretty hopeless. After all, as long as Lucinda knew the secret of the curse and she could keep the two jewels separated, she could spread the word to other ghosts that they could take on real bodies too. And that wouldn't leave any room on Earth for the people already here and alive, would it?

Mom gave her a smile. "Don't be discouraged, Molly," she said. "There's really no point. Let's not think about how this will turn out. Let's just think about what we have to do: One, find the elephant. Two, find the necklace and take out the sapphire. Three, get the ring from Reggie and take out the emerald. Four, put the sapphire and the emerald back in the elephant, and five, put the elephant away in a very safe place, forever. That's all. The rest is irrelevant."

When you put it like that, it did sound much simpler. More doable, somehow. That was Mom. All action. Why worry about something that hadn't happened yet? And Molly was usually like that too. And, she realized, she'd better be like that again or she'd be useless. She straightened her drooping shoulders and said, "Quite right, Mom. As the Brits would say, stiff upper lip, right?"

"Righty ho," her mom said. "And full speed ahead!"

CHAPTER SIX
Hunting the Hidden

So full speed ahead it was. Molly finished her lunch, helped clean up the paper plates and cups, and hurried into the car along with her father and her brother. Her mom said she'd stay behind in the cottage and wait for Reggie, who was driving himself up from the airport, and also for Granddad, who had gone off somewhere into the ether or the astral plane or whatever it was. Of course, he might show up at any minute. Maybe with some ghostly friends in tow. Maybe with their great-great-great-granddad Maurice. You never knew with ghosts.

The drive into Oxford was very pretty—the fields were so green, and the high hedges on both sides of the road were beautifully lush and green, too, even if they were so close to the very narrow road that every time another car came driving toward them Molly was convinced she might soon be a ghost herself. The roads here in England were all so narrow that the mirrors on the sides of the cars swivelled in so that they wouldn't be sheered off by cars passing in the other direction.

Soon, thankfully, they were off the small road and onto a larger one. They drove by a huge empty factory, and then by a big round windowless building about ten storeys high that her dad called a gasometer. It was where they used to store all the natural gas before it went out to heat buildings and things, Dad said, and it looked sort of like a giant and very dirty grain silo. They passed a Tesco's and other stores in the mall. The street they found the auction house on some blocks later was a combination of old houses and old houses that had been converted into Indian restaurants.

People in Oxford must sure like curry a lot, Adam thought as his dad parked the car. He could kind of go for some curry himself right now. That would definitely take away any lingering taste of animal head parts.

In between two of the curry places was a small shop with a sign in old-fashioned lettering: Messinger and Messinger and Sons.

Adam and Molly followed their dad to the front door. When Dad opened the door, a little bell dinged.

Stuffed with huge birdcages and lamps with tassels and paintings of ugly old men with beards, the shop looked like something out of an old black-and-white horror movie, Molly thought. It was the kind of place where at any minute a corpse might topple out of a grandfather clock.

A small round man hurried out from behind a long counter and came toward them. He had a small round head, and was dressed in a flamboyant reddish-brown tweed suit that Molly thought wasn't at all suitable for a dark shop filled to the brim with old stuff. He looked more like a car salesman than an antique dealer.

"May I help you?" he asked, rubbing his hands together. "Markus Messinger, at your service."

Molly's dad held out his hand and the small man shook it enthusiastically.

"My name is Tim Barnett," Dad said. "My mother was Dora—over at The Oaks in—"

"Toot Baldon," both kids chimed in together, then grinned when they realized they'd said the same thing at the same time.

"Ah, charming," Mr. Messinger said, giving Molly and Adam a small nod. "Nice to see the youngsters know where they are."

"Toot Baldon!" they repeated, grins becoming broader.

Dad gave them both a look.

"Yes, very nice," said Dad. "We just arrived from overseas this morning."

"Oh," said Mr. Messinger, "I see. But you were mentioning Dora Barnett? From Toot—"

"Baldon!" Adam and Molly said. They both broke out into giggles.

"Jet lag," said Dad through pursed lips. "As I was saying," and he threw them another glare, "Dora Barnett was my mother. I arranged for you to sell her things last year?"

"Yes, indeed," said Mr. Messinger. "I remember the sale quite well, Mr. Barnett. Your mother had an amazingly diverse selection of things. A lot of useless tat, I'm afraid, but there were some fine Wilson Hepple horse paintings, and a number of interesting Victorian porcelain bedpans."

"Yes," said Dad, "I think there were."

"Not to mention a bronze Georgian marine chronometer in excellent condition! And an Imari vase in the shape of a heron! And so many other fine things, too! That sale took an entire day, and it attracted buyers from all over the south of England. There was even a dealer from Milwaukee in America, who came over for it especially!"

Great, thought Adam. That meant the elephant might be almost anywhere. Even Milwaukee, of all places.

Or maybe no one had bought it and it was still somewhere in the very crowded shop. As Adam gazed around the clutter, he crossed his fingers behind his back.

"The thing is," said Dad, "there were a few things

that were, uh, left behind in the house by accident—things we didn't actually want to sell."

"Oh?" said Mr. Messinger, with a look of consternation.

"Here," Dad interrupted as he dug into his pocket. "I've got that list of yours. Ah, here it is." He waved the papers at Mr. Messinger.

"But, Mr. Barnett," said Mr. Messinger. "I can't—"

"There," Dad said, unfolding the list and pointing at it. "That elephant. It was a mistake. Turns out it's an old family heirloom and we desperately want it back."

"Desperately?" The man said. He seemed to disapprove of the word, as if he himself would never be so emotional. "I'd like to help you, Mr. Barnett, and I will—if I can. But, well, an insignificant little trinket like that—you really can't expect me to remember where it might have gone. If the object has been sold, well then, I'm afraid—"

"But *has* it been sold?" Molly interrupted impatiently.

"Yes," her dad added. "Has it? I'm prepared to give you a fair price if we can get it back in our hands."

Mr. Messinger's face brightened at the mention of a fair price. "I can see it means a lot to you, Mr. Barnett," he said. "As well it might—a valuable old curio like that."

Adam noticed that the elephant had suddenly become more valuable now that money was involved.

"Give me a moment," said Mr. Messinger, rubbing his hands together again. "I'll need to check my records."

He turned and moved through the crowded aisles toward the back of the shop, the Barnetts following behind much more slowly as they manoeuvred their way past piles of breakable objects.

Not an elephant in sight, thought Adam as he tried to make sense of all the clutter.

Molly expected Mr. Messinger to find an old filing cabinet and then take hours sifting through the aging yellowed papers in it. Instead, he settled on a chair in front of a small desk in a corner, a little antique-looking round desk, but there was a sleek silver laptop sitting on it. He flipped it open and his fingers started to fly.

"Eureka!" he said after a brief moment. "Here it is! Oh, dear. I'm afraid you're out of luck, Mr. Barnett. We did indeed sell that little elephant."

Great, thought Adam again. Why would anybody want to buy such a thing? Why did they buy it? It wasn't fair.

"Could you tell us who bought it?" asked Dad.

Mr. Messinger turned around, looking grim. "Really, Mr. Barnett," he said, "we here at Messinger and Messinger and Sons haven't been in business for the last two hundred and thirty-four years because we give out confidential information. Our customers have a right to their privacy."

"But we really do need to get it back," said Adam

desperately. "We really, really do!"

"My son is right, Mr. Messinger," Dad added. "We really do. Couldn't you, maybe, bend your rules a little? If we could have a name and address, perhaps—or even just a phone number?"

Mr. Messinger shook his head firmly. "Definitely not. It's our tradition, Mr. Barnett. Messinger and Messinger and Sons is nothing if it is not its traditions. Nothing at all."

It's a pity Mom isn't here, thought Molly. She'd have the information out of him in two seconds flat.

But Mom wasn't there. And Dad was just sputtering.

Moving behind her dad's back, Molly grabbed Adam's arm. "Do something to distract him," she whispered in his ear.

Adam understood. He nodded then quickly looked around again. His gaze settled on a large china statue of a mermaid holding a fish above her head, apparently about to drop it into her mouth. The mermaid was standing on a rickety little table about halfway down the aisle.

"Wow!" Adam exclaimed in a loud voice, pointing at it. "Look at that! It must weigh a ton! I wonder if I can lift it!"

And he headed over to the mermaid.

It was amazing how quickly Mr. Messinger could move when he really wanted to.

"No, no," he screamed as he rushed past Molly and her dad toward Adam. "Sevres, that is! It's worth fifty thousand pounds, that is!"

Golly, thought Adam as he pretended to try to lift the statue. Fifty thousand pounds! Who knew I had such excellent taste?

Molly wasted no time. As Mr. Messinger focused his attention on Adam, she scooted over to the little desk, found the information they wanted on the computer screen, and quickly memorized it. By the time Mr. Messinger reached Adam, she was back beside her father again.

"I'm sorry, Mr. Barnett," said Mr. Messinger as he pried Adam's hands off the statue and gave him an angry look. "Tradition is tradition, and policy is policy. The best I can do is contact the purchaser for you and ask her if she'd be willing to give it up. Can you leave a number where you can be reached?"

The phone at the cottage wasn't hooked up, so Dad gave him his cell number. "But," he added, "it really is urgent, Mr. Messinger, and I can't see why—"

"Thank you, Mr. Messinger," Molly said, as she grabbed her dad's arm and began pushing him out of the shop. "We really appreciate your help!"

"Molly, what are you doing?" her dad said as he struggled against her. Adam rushed over, grabbed his dad's other arm, and in a moment they were all out on the street, the little bell jingling to announce their sudden departure.

"I looked at the computer," she said as soon as they were outside. "She lives right here in Oxford."

Dad looked at her with approval. "Good work, Molly."

"I helped, too," said Adam. "Why do you think I pretended to lift that statue?"

"Well, thank you too then, Adam," Dad said. "What's the address, Molly?"

"100 Manor Place."

"Manor Place. Hmm. I think I know where that is—down St. Cross, near St. Catharine's College."

"What are we waiting for?" said Molly.

And they all clambered back into the car.

CHAPTER SEVEN
The Haunted House

As Dad made his way through the narrow streets, trying to remember to stay on the left and cursing when the tires bumped into the curb, he turned on the radio.

Molly sighed. Her Dad could barely survive an hour without getting a news fix. He was always switching back and forth between the news feeds he had on his computer desktop and the TV news channels, and he hated public holidays when nobody went in to their offices and so almost nothing new or bad happened.

"The cause of the fire in central London was not clear," the announcer said, "but investigators said it may have been set by a homeless man seen in the vicinity earlier carrying a lighted torch, begging for pennies, and asking directions to Westminster. Meanwhile, reports of strange behaviour continue to come in from all over the United Kingdom. In Liverpool, a group of teenaged girls claim that two drunken football fans carrying wooden clubs and dressed only in fur pelts accosted them outside the Layton Square Mall, and shouted at them in what sounded like German or Danish, and then grabbed their purses and ran off. No German or Danish football team was playing in Liverpool at the time. Back in London, two stockbrokers in the City claim they were nearly run through by two sword-wielding men dressed in costumes and directed by a woman in an ornate ball gown who laughed and then shouted, 'Let zem eat *gâteau*!' In Yorkshire, a man identifying himself as Mr. S. Todd, esquire, and carrying a bloodstained cleaver asked to see the meat manager of a local Sainsbury's. He then offered her a good selection of fresh meat pies, to be produced on demand. 'Finest in London,' he claimed before escaping from the security guard who tried to restrain him, 'and now the finest in Yorkshire!' And this just in: another wild-eyed, long-haired fellow dressed in what appeared to be early nineteenth-century clothing was arrested for disturbing the peace in Brighton. He interrupted a beach wedding near the pier by waving a walking stick at the ocean and shouting, 'Roll on, thou deep and dark blue ocean, roll!'"

"'Ten thousand fleets sweep over thee in vain,'" said Dad. "I know that poem—I studied it at university. Romantic Poetry 205. It's by Lord Byron."

"Contacted by the BBC," the announcer went on, "Professor of Sociology Rosemary Heathe of the University of East Anglia reminded us that there is a full moon tonight. 'Incidents of this sort often increase in these circumstances,' said Professor Heathe, who added that she very much doubted it was worth worrying about. 'I'm sure they're all perfectly harmless,' she said. In other news, the oil-producing emirates——"

"Dad," said Molly, turning down the radio, "this sounds just like what we've been worried about. It couldn't be, could it?"

"It could be," Adam said. And then after a pause he added glumly, "it's started."

"This is horrible," his dad said, swerving to avoid a mailbox standing just at the edge of the sidewalk.

"So these really are people from history, right?" Adam said. "Lucinda has begun to let ghosts know they can return to their Earthly bodies—and some of them are already doing it!"

Dad nodded. "That must be what's happening."

So far, the returned ghosts sounded pretty harmless. But once they got used to being alive again . . . Adam shuddered at the possibilities.

"Which means," said Molly, "that time is running out. Let's get moving!"

"Let's not be too hasty, kidlets," said Dad. "That professor may turn out to be right. It may just be the full moon or something."

But he stepped on the gas anyway, and the car hurtled through the narrow streets, scaring anyone foolish enough to be out on the road at the wrong time. They lost a wheel cover when they hit a pedestrian crossing sign, but they were at 100 Manor Place within minutes.

But after he stopped the car, Dad sat there, seemingly at a loss.

"What do I say to her?" he asked.

"You could start by saying, 'Hello, Ms. Garryty-Smythe-Lowing," Molly said. "Because her name is Martha Garryty-Smythe-Lowing. Hard to forget a name like that," she added with a giggle.

"Garryty-Smythe-Lowing," Adam repeated. "That's almost as good as Toot Baldon."

"Toot Baldon," said Molly.

"Garryty-Smythe-Lowing," said Adam.

"This is not helping," said Dad. "Seriously, how am I going to talk her into giving back the elephant?"

"Couldn't we just tell her the truth?" said Adam.

"Oh, sure," said Molly. "I mean, really, Adam. A total stranger rings your doorbell to tell you that a lot of very scary ghosts are going to be coming back to life unless you hand over some dumb little ornament you bought at an auction sale. What would you do?"

"Well," said Adam, "If it was me——"

"I know what *you* would do, Adam," said Molly. "I meant, what would a normal person do?"

"If you two don't stop squabbling," said Dad, "I'm

going to make you wait here in the car."

"Sorry," Adam and Molly mumbled at the same time.

"Good," said Dad. "You can come along—but you have to promise to let me do the talking."

"Okay," said Adam.

"Sure," said Molly. "But what will you say?"

"As little as possible," said Dad. "Let's just keep our fingers crossed."

The house was in a row of houses all joined together, with neat gardens surrounded by low brick walls, and cheerfully painted front doors, most of them light blue. Soon the three of them were standing in front of one of the blue doors, Molly and Adam waiting behind their dad as he used the gleaming brass knocker.

A moment passed, and then a woman opened the door. She wore a round pair of glasses with lenses at least an inch thick, a long cardigan covering a long grey skirt, and sensible laced-up leather shoes. Her grey hair was in a bun. Molly thought she looked exactly like a librarian in some British movie—the kind who seems totally harmless, but ends up being the murderer who poisoned fourteen innocent victims for folding up the corners of pages in library books.

"May I help?" she said, peering at them.

"Yes," said Dad, "I believe you can. I mean, I hope you can. My name is Tim Barnett and this is my daughter, Molly and my son, Adam."

"How do you do?" said Martha Garryty-Smythe-Lowing, looking as if she had no interest whatsoever in how they did, or in anything else about them.

"I'm here with my family from overseas," Dad continued, "staying in Toot Baldon where my parents used to live at The Oaks."

"Indeed?" the woman said with more interest. "The Oaks? A nice little house, The Oaks is. Well preserved, as it should be."

"My mother passed away last year," Dad continued, "and we're here now to . . . to . . ."

"To finish going through the house," Molly said helpfully.

Dad quickly gave her a disapproving look then turned back again.

"To finish going through the house," he told Martha Garryty-Smythe-Lowing. "Anyway, last year I hired Messinger and Messinger to sell the items we didn't want. But well, it seems that there was . . ."

"An oversight," Molly prompted.

"Yes," Dad said with another unhappy look, "an oversight. And some items were sold that should not have been."

"Ah," said the woman with a nod, "I see. Interesting. Can you show me some identification papers, Mr. Barnett?"

"Uh, yes, I suppose so," said Dad. He took his passport from his pocket and handed it to her.

"This seems to be in order," she said as she looked carefully through its pages. "Although it doesn't really flatter your hair, does it? And you can swear that you really are the son of the owner of that Renaissance house in Toot Baldon? The Oaks?"

"Why, yes," Dad said, surprised. "I spent my own childhood there, in fact."

"Cross your heart and hope to die?"

"Uh," said Dad even more surprised. "I suppose so. I mean, yes, cross my heart and hope to die." He crossed his heart as he said it.

"Good," she said, smiling. "One can't be too careful these days, can one? You'd better come in and sit down."

Molly followed her Dad and Martha Garryty-Smythe-Lowing through the door, wondering if everyone in the world had gone completely batty. Molly herself hadn't asked anyone to cross their heart and hope to die for years—not since grade one, when she grew up enough to stop believing in Santa Claus and the Tooth Fairy. And Martha Garryty-Smythe-Lowing had seemed like such a nice, sensible person, too. Molly hoped that they wouldn't find a convention of green Martians sitting inside. If there were, Adam would never ever let her forget it.

But there were no Martians, thank goodness. It was just a comfy-looking, but very overcrowded sitting room, with chintz sofas and knick-knacks laid out on every free surface.

It looked a lot like Gram's house used to look.

In fact, Molly thought she could recognize some of Gram's things. The little silver duck wearing a knitted scarf and beanie on the table in front of the sofa, for instance—it was either Gram's, or one exactly like it. And how many scarf-and-beanie-wearing silver ducks could there be in the world? How many people would actually want such a silly thing?

Anyway, it was clear that Martha Garryty-Smythe-Lowing had been very busy at that auction sale. The elephant might be somewhere near them right now!

She gestured toward the small sofa. Dad sat down and patted the seats on either side of him for Molly and Adam to sit as well.

"I assume there is an article that I purchased that you wish to retrieve?" Martha Garryty-Smythe-Lowing asked.

"Yes," said Dad, happily feeling that things were going much more smoothly than he had hoped. "That's it exactly!"

"And what might the item in question be?"

"It's a plain sort of elephant," Dad said. "Carved in ivory. Nothing much to look at, but it has sentimental value, you see." He waited and when she didn't answer he added, "You did buy that ivory elephant? You do have it?"

"Well now, Mr. Barnett," she said, "the thing is, you aren't the first person to inquire about that item."

"What?" Molly exclaimed.

Martha Garryty-Smythe-Lowing gave Molly a severe look. She obviously did not approve of emotion of any kind, especially from young people.

"As I was saying," she went on, "a few days ago—last Monday, I believe it was, because I was baking coconut toasties for the ladies auxiliary tea at St. Mary's, and the tea was Monday evening, so yes, it was Monday. Last Monday afternoon, a rather strange woman appeared on my doorstep unannounced, much as you have today." She paused for a moment to make it clear that she did not approve of such behaviour.

"As I was saying, this woman also asked about this very same elephant," she continued. "I really am most upset with Mr. Messinger for releasing information about me to total strangers. I am an excellent customer of many years standing, and he would not want to lose my business."

I bet he wouldn't, Adam thought, glancing around the room. Martha Garryty-Smythe-Lowing obviously loved to buy antiques.

"In our case, Ma'am," said Dad. "I can assure you that Mr. Messinger is not responsible for our appearance here."

Anything but, thought Adam. If Mr. Messinger knew they were here, he'd be having a fit.

"Indeed?" Martha Garryty-Smythe-Lowing said through pursed lips, giving him a piercing glance over the top of her glasses. "Then how did you know where I lived?"

"Uh, well, I—"

"It's a long story, ma'am," said Molly. "But you were saying something about a woman?"

Once more, Martha Garryty-Smythe-Lowing gave Molly a dark look, almost as dark as the one Dad was giving her.

"I mean," Molly continued, "I'm sure you're very busy, I mean, what with the ladies auxiliary and all."

"And the cocoanut toasties," Adam added before he even realized he was doing it. But they did sound good. And as it happened, he was feeling a little hungry.

"If you could just tell us about her," Molly continued, "we could be on our way in no time."

"Yes," said Martha Garryty-Smythe-Lowing in a grim voice. "You could, couldn't you? Well, as I was saying, this woman knocked on my door, bold as brass, and demanded that I return her property to her."

"Her property?" Dad said.

"Yes. A small carved ivory elephant. Which I did purchase and did have in the house when she arrived."

Molly realized she had stopped breathing.

"This woman insisted that the elephant was hers," Martha Garryty-Smythe-Lowing went on, "although she could offer no explanation as to how it ended up in The Oaks sale. Perhaps you might help me with that?"

"I can assure, you, ma'am, that the elephant had

been in our family for generations. I have evidence on paper for it, if you should wish to see it," Dad said, the colour draining from his face, perhaps realizing that Lucinda might have beat them to it.

"I don't think that will be necessary. Not that I'm surprised—I knew there was something fishy about that woman."

"You did?" Molly asked, her emotions careening from despair to hope.

"Indeed I did. For one thing, she was dressed oddly and she offered no explanation of why that would be. Never even mentioned it, just expected me to take it for granted that somebody might come to my door wearing an old-fashioned black skirt with a white apron over it. And I might add that the apron was no longer really white, but quite grubby. She looked like a servant from the turn of the last century, and not a very tidy one. Frilly white cap, you know?"

Molly let out what must have sounded like a squeak. Now it was confirmed all right. Definitely Lucinda.

"Excuse me?" said Martha Garryty-Smythe-Lowing.

"Nothing," said Molly. "It's just that—"

"She isn't someone you know, is she? You're not in this together?" A new thought occurred to her. "What- ever this is."

"No, Ma'am," said Dad, "I can assure you that we're not in this together."

"Anything but," said Adam.

73

"At the time," Martha Garryty-Smythe-Lowing said, "I thought she might have been on some kind of scavenger hunt—a college student, perhaps, except she certainly didn't seem like a college student. But then, you know, it's so hard to tell these days. They seem to let just about anybody in, even at the best colleges. Even at Kings, where my own dear departed husband Aloysius was a choir boy. Do you know who she is?"

"We might," said Dad, "but I can assure you that she has no right to that elephant. As I said, it's an old family heirloom—and if you could bring yourself to part with it, well, we'd be really grateful. And of course, I'd be happy to pay you back what you paid for it—and more, too, for your trouble."

"That's certainly more than what that odd woman offered," said Martha Garryty-Smythe-Lowing. "She actually stuck her boot in the doorway and kept insisting that it really belonged to her and demanded it back. So I kicked her foot and slammed the door in her face!"

"Then——" Adam could hardly believe their luck, "then you still have the elephant?"

"I most certainly do," she replied. "The funny thing was, I never heard a peep out of her after that. No protests at all, although she did certainly seem the kind who would protest. And when I looked out the window a few minutes later, she was gone. Good riddance to bad rubbish, I say!"

"So," said Dad, "might you consider selling the elephant back to me? It meant a great deal to my parents. And—"

"My gram used to let me hold that elephant while she sang lullabies to me when I was a baby," said Adam, squeezing his eyes shut hard in order to make tears appear. "It means so, so much to me."

Molly had to hand it him. He was very convincing. He was even beginning to cry.

"Me, too," she added. "I love Gram's elephant. I'd be so, so pleased to have it back again." She tried, unsuccessfully, for a few tears of her own.

"Well," said Martha Garryty-Smythe-Lowing, "I have to admit it; I'm not really all that fond of it after all. Up close, it's not really the most attractive piece. It has no eyes, you understand."

"Yes," said Dad, "We do."

Boy, do we ever, thought Adam. And that means it is our elephant.

"Mr. Messinger assured me that it could be restored," Martha Garryty-Smythe-Lowing added, "but really, I'm not sure I like the thing enough to spend that much on it. Although—" she suddenly seemed to remember they were going to offer money for it—"it is very old, of course, a genuine antique, almost priceless. Let me go and fetch it, and then perhaps we can talk about it."

"That was much easier than I thought it would be," said Dad as Martha Garryty-Smythe-Lowing left them behind in the sitting room. Seconds later, she rushed back into the room.

"I don't understand it!" she exclaimed. "It's gone! It was sitting right there on the left side of my dresser, right between the Royal Doulton balloon seller and the Mexican castanets—and now it's not there anymore!"

Lucinda, thought Molly grimly. They ought to have known she wouldn't give up so easily.

"Perhaps," said Dad, "you just moved it yourself—while you were dusting or something? Could it be somewhere else?"

"I assure you, Mr. Barnett," said Martha Garryty-Smythe-Lowing, "I have an excellent memory. I did not move it. I am certain of it. But I suppose I will look around. Just to be sure." She headed off once more.

"It must have been Lucinda, right?" said Adam.

"Yes, for sure," said Molly.

"But how would she get in without Martha What-sherface knowing?" asked Dad.

"Maybe she turned herself back into a ghost again," Adam suggested, "and went through the wall."

"Not logical, Adam," said Dad, "because as a ghost she couldn't carry a real object like the elephant."

"She probably just came back when Martha was out and climbed in through a window or something," said Molly impatiently. "How she got it doesn't matter.

The important thing is that she's got it. What a disaster!"

Martha Garryty-Smythe-Lowing re-entered the room, a very grim expression on her face. "It is nowhere to be found," she said. "I fear foul play."

Then she stared at them, her eyes narrowed. "Are you sure you have no connection to that strange woman? This isn't some silly TV show, is it? There aren't any cameras?"

"No, Ma'am," said Dad as he rose to his feet. "I can assure you, it's not a TV show. I only wish it were. But we won't take up any more of you time now. You've been very kind. Come, kidlets."

He handed her one of his cards, and added, "Here's my cellphone number. Don't hesitate to call if you happen on the elephant."

"Or if that woman comes back again," said Adam.

"Back? Here?" said Martha Garryty-Smythe-Lowing as she took the card. "She had better not dare!"

She shut the door firmly behind them as they left. But when they got in the car and were all buckled up, they had no idea of where to go or what to do next.

"That elephant could be anywhere by now," said Adam.

"Or even worse, said Molly. "It could be nowhere."

"Nowhere?" said Adam. "What do you mean?"

"I mean," said Molly, "that Lucinda might have al-ready destroyed it. Wouldn't that be the obvious thing for her to do?"

"Yes," said Dad. "You're right, Molly, it would. If she wants to stop us from putting the jewels into the eyes, then destroying it as soon as she got her hands on it would be the wisest thing for her to do."

"Unless——" Adam began, and then stopped.

"Unless what?" said Molly.

"I don't know, really," said Adam. "Something about that poem—the one about what would happen if the eyes came out of the elephant."

"What about it?" Molly insisted.

For a moment, Adam was silent. "I'm not sure," he said finally. "I'll have to think about it."

Dad sighed. "Meanwhile," he said, "we'll just have to hope the elephant is still in one piece. But where to look for it or what to do now—well, I have no idea."

"Me either," said Molly. "Let's just head back to Toot Baldon. Maybe Granddad or Mom will have an idea."

Just as Dad was about to put the key in the ignition, his phone rang.

"Hello," he said. "Reggie? Is that you?" He listened for a moment. "She did what?" Dad swore. "Where?"

Molly looked at Adam, who was already imagining the worst. Maybe Reggie had been in an accident on the M1. Or maybe he had been spirited away by ghosts and was trapped in some dungeon where they were tormenting him. Adam had seen a piece on CNN last week about a judge who had sentenced kids who were playing their music too loud in their cars; he'd forced them to listen to four hours straight of Barry Manilow and Dora the Explorer music. No doubt ghosts and nasty spirits had heard that report as well, and were Dora-ing and Manilow-ing Reggie right now. What could be worse? Adam shuddered.

"You're breaking up!" Dad yelled into the phone. He paused. "Reggie?" He hung up, swearing yet again. "The phone went dead. I think Reggie is in trouble, but I'm not sure how, or where. And I'm not sure how we can help him."

His phone rang again. "Reggie?" he shouted into it. "Where are you?" He listened a moment. "Oh, Lily, it's you. Reggie's in trouble. Yes? Yes. Oh, he called you, too, did he? Did he say where?"

"Reggie is in trouble!" a voice in the back seat declared.

It was Granddad, who had suddenly appeared.

"We need to help him!" Granddad shouted. "Now! Drive!"

CHAPTER EIGHT
A Haunting Verse

"I'll call you back later, Lily," said Dad. "My father's here, and he seems to know where Reggie is." He clicked off the phone and handed it to Molly.

"Where are we going, Dad?"

"You just drive, Timmie," Granddad said. "I'll give you the directions. Reggie is stuck in a dungeon."

Just like Adam had imagined! Now he was really worried. Was he psychic suddenly, or what?

"Turn left here," Granddad instructed. "Actually, it's not really a dungeon. In fact, it's my old school, New College."

"My old school, too," said Dad.

"Really?" said Granddad. "Following in your old man's footsteps? How flattering! At any rate, as you no doubt remember, there is a place under the chapel we used to call the 'dungeon,' back in the old days when I was a student and Gerry and the Pacemakers were all the rage. It's not really a dungeon, though—it's a crypt."

Well, that didn't sound too bad, Adam thought. It wasn't really a dungeon. And how bad could a new college be? Not like the really ancient colleges they were beginning to drive by now—all medieval and ivy-covered and scary looking, the kind of places that ghosts would haunt or where vampires and Franken-stein monsters would hang out. Adam would have thought they'd gone through a time warp if it weren't for the occasional McDonald's and KFC, not to men-tion a few more curry restaurants. And it was a new college, he told himself—and it wasn't a dungeon, it was something else. A 'crick' or something.

"What's a crypt?" asked Molly.

"A place where they keep the bones of dead people," said Granddad.

Oh great, thought Adam. It's not a dungeon, oh no—it's even worse than a dungeon.

"Step on it, Timmie," said Granddad. "Reggie's in real trouble."

Adam just bet he was. Being battered by scary skel-etons, maybe.

"I'm going as fast as I can," their dad replied. "We don't want to get stopped for speeding, do we?"

As they hurtled through the narrow streets, Molly, holding on for dear life, still had time to wonder what was happening to Reggie.

"Who has him prisoner?" she asked. "And why?"

"Now a right," Granddad answered. "It's Lucinda, of course. Who else? Although Reggie didn't realize it was her when she ran out into the middle of the road just as he was driving into Oxford. When he managed to stop just before hitting her, she demanded that he hand over the ring. He refused, of course, and she got really angry and told him there were ways to make him talk. Somehow—I'm not quite clear how—she made him drive to New College and then locked him up in the crypt."

"That is not good news," said Molly.

"Poor Reggie," Adam agreed. He could think of all kinds of ways Lucinda might try to make the poor guy talk. Many of them involved insects and none was the least bit pleasant.

"Poor Reggie, sure," Molly said, "and we have to try to help him. But also the fact that she bothered to kidnap Reggie so she could get the stone means that she knows for sure about the elephant and is trying to stop us from replacing the jewels in its eyes. She must have figured out the curse!"

"Oh, yeah, the poem." Adam began to recite it.

" 'Together forever
The world all unsevered
The dangers all weathered.
But apart, and the heart

Of the world will unfurl
And chaos shall come
And the loud shall be dumb
And the living undone
And the dead shall return
To the bodies they left
And the world shall be cleft
And bereft.'"

He thought for a moment about what it meant. The two eyes, the sapphire and the emerald, the Morning Eye and the Evening Eye, had been removed from the elephant. They were apart, so the world would unfurl, and the dead could return to the bodies they left. And now Lucinda knew it, and could act on it.

"You're right," he finally said. "That is bad news."

"If she has both the ring and the pendant," Molly added, "and can keep them out of the elephant, she can come and go as she pleases and destroy the world at the same time."

"I'm still wondering why she wouldn't just want to destroy the elephant," Adam said. "It's something about that poem, something—"

"What I'm wondering," said Dad, "is how on Earth she got Reggie into the basement of New College. Wouldn't people notice? Isn't there a porter on duty?"

"And how did you find him, Granddad?" Molly asked.

"I could hear him calling for help," Granddad answered. "Not literally, of course—it came to me while I was out there in the ether on the astral plane, checking to see if any suspicious ghosts were around. I also wanted to see if I could find our ancestors—Maurice, for instance—or if I could find out anything about the little boy John. Anyway," Granddad continued, "I heard Reggie, faintly at first but then more clearly. It's the first time I've heard a still living person call me when I've been out there."

"How strange," Molly said.

Adam found himself remembering last summer, when they'd first met Reggie. Back then, they'd worried that he, too, might be a ghost. They soon learned he wasn't—or so it had seemed. But if Granddad was hearing him now in that place where he met up with other ghosts . . .

"It's rather puzzling," Granddad said. "Reggie really shouldn't have access to that place. I wonder if it's because of the connection our families have. We're on the same wavelength, as young people like to say."

It sort of made sense. Adam wondered if that was why he had also suddenly pictured Reggie in trouble—in a dungeon.

But why were their families connected? It was something to do with the elephant, obviously—the elephant and the jewels and the curse.

And the poem. There was something about that

poem, about the living being undone. . . .

"But how did Lucinda lure him down there?" Molly asked, feeling quite creeped out by the whole thing. After all, if Lucinda could imprison a huge fellow like Reggie, what chance did a skinny thirteen-year-old girl have? Or her eleven-year-old brother, for that matter. It's true she was taking karate, and once last month in class she'd managed to topple Jeff Spender, who was a great, huge hulk of a guy. So that might help—but would it, against a ghost? If Molly kicked Lucinda, Lucinda might just disappear and then pop up again somewhere else. Not a fair fight at all!

"We're almost there," said Granddad. "You just have to turn left here."

"I can't!" Dad shouted as the car screeched to a sudden halt. "There's a barrier!"

Molly lurched forward, her seatbelt tugging at her waist. The car came to a stop just inches away from an iron gate sort of thing, blocking off almost the entire street.

"What's that doing there?" said Granddad. "It must be Lucinda up to her tricks again."

"Not this time, Granddad," said Molly, remembering earlier trips into Oxford when she was a child and her dad had been swearing just like he was now. "It's because no private cars are allowed to drive into the middle of Oxford—to stop traffic congestion around the colleges."

"That's ridiculous, Molly," said Granddad. "It wasn't there when I was here last. Let's see, I had a class that day, it must have been—"

"Last century, Granddad," said Adam. "About thirty years ago? Remember?" Poor Granddad was always forgetting that he was dead—and had been dead for a long time. It must be awfully confusing to be a ghost.

"Never mind about that now," said Molly as she opened the door and stepped out of the car. "Reggie is in trouble! Let's get moving!"

In a few seconds, Adam and their dad had joined her. They raced down the street, Granddad hovering anxiously alongside them and shouting out directions. They soon arrived at an archway leading into New College.

"This way," Granddad called, "right in here!"

"Halt!" a voice shouted as they ran under the arch.

Molly turned to see a small, skinny man standing beside the gate. He looked very upset.

"Come back here immediately," he said. "No one can come into the quadrangle except masters and students. Unless you have an appointment?"

Adam, Molly, and their dad froze, cowed for the moment by the authority in the man's voice.

How, thought Adam, could they explain why they needed to get in? "We believe there's a prisoner locked up in your dungeon, sir." Yeah, sure, that would really go over well. They'd probably all end up in the dungeon themselves.

"This is ridiculous," said Granddad, popping into view right in front of the little man, whose eyes suddenly widened into an uncomprehending gaze. "I have every right to be here, and these people are my guests. Honestly! You porters need to show more respect for the masters!"

"I'm used to pranks by undergraduates," the little man said calmly, "but people of your age should know better. Now off with you."

Adam found this interesting—this fellow could see Granddad, as could the person at immigration. Was the curse making all ghosts more visible, even if they weren't in their old bodies?

"Fine," said Granddad impatiently. "If you want me to be off, then I'm off. Here I go, right now."

Adam had to contain a laugh as Granddad disappeared and appeared again. The look on the porter's face was priceless. Molly, on the other hand, was a little worried about his heart. He was beginning to look a little pale and she didn't want them to be responsible for the poor fellow going into cardiac arrest.

"Now listen to me," Granddad continued, "and listen carefully. There is a man being held prisoner in the crypt. If we don't go down and rescue him right now, the entire world is in peril. Would you like to be responsible for the world as we know it coming to an end? Of course not! So my family and I are going down to the crypt. Right now. And you, Sir, are not going to stop us. Correct?"

"Bloody right I'm not going to stop you," the man said with some bluster as the colour returned to his cheeks. "You are obviously mad. Completely and totally bonkers. Go right down to the crypt, please do. Make yourself welcome. Have a glass of sherry, maybe, or some salsa and tortilla chips—there's probably a Mexican restaurant opening up there now, to serve all the bones. I, meanwhile, shall be calling the police!" He moved toward his little office.

"Not a bad idea," said Molly, relieved that the fellow had recovered so well. "We can probably use the police."

"I agree, Molly," said Dad. He called after the porter, "Please do call the police. We'd be most grateful. And tell them it's an emergency."

Then he turned to his father. "Let's go, Pop, kidlets. Which way?"

"It's down here," said Granddad. "Through the cloisters."

CHAPTER NINE
Dead Knight Haunting

Granddad, Dad, Molly, and Adam hurried through the archway into a large, green space surrounded by buildings. Old buildings.

Adam was confused.

"I thought you said *New* College," he said to his granddad.

"Yes," Granddad said with pride in his voice "It's really St. Mary College, you see, but it's a few years newer than Oriel College, which is also called St. Mary College—so that's why this one's called the New College."

"Oh," said Adam, wondering why anyone wanted to give two different colleges the same name. "It sure doesn't look very new."

"Well, it's only been here for about six hundred years—but less than Oriel, you see? But I suppose it could do with a bit of a scrubbing."

They ran down what Adam could only describe as an outside hallway with an arched roof overhead and arched windows with no glass. When they reached a set of stone steps that led downward, Granddad told them that they were very close indeed. Adam did not like the look of where they were heading. He hoped that being together would help if they were to get into a fight with Lucinda.

Along with Molly and his dad, Adam followed Granddad's voice down the steep stone steps and then down a dark corridor with only the light from the outdoors to guide them, and there wasn't much of that. A door on the left, near the end of the corridor, was shaking. Someone was banging on it so hard it rattled, even though Adam thought it must be one of those old doors too thick to really budge.

Adam watched as his dad tried the handle.

"Locked," he said.

"And no way to unlock it without a key," Granddad added.

Adam thought for a moment about rushing back up the stairs and asking the guy at the gate. Fat chance— even if he had a key he wouldn't give it to Adam.

But maybe the police would be there soon.

Adam could hear muffled shouts coming from behind the locked door.

Molly yelled as loud as she could. "Reggie! Reggie, we're here!"

She heard a muted reply.

"I'll go keep him company until the police get here," Granddad said, as he blinked out.

Adam was very relieved that they had discovered Reggie. After all, he could have died down here before anyone even realized he was trapped.

But at least it looked like it was going to be a simple rescue operation. As soon as the police arrived—

"Out! Out, intruders! Begone!"

Molly had been so intent on listening for Reggie that the shout made her jump straight into the air. She turned to see a man in a metal suit and hat—like the ones Molly had often seen in movies and TV shows about olden-day knights. But this man certainly wasn't a knight in shining armour. His armour was very dirty, smeared with blood stains and disturbing spots of goo, and he was moving toward them, sword drawn.

"You dare to trespass?" he bellowed. "Death will be your punishment or my name is not Sir Eustace Winslet!"

Dad pushed the children behind him and started to back away. As he did, Granddad appeared in front of all of them. "Go away," he said calmly to the ghost. "You don't belong here anymore. You're dead!"

Sir Eustace shouted, "Not me, varlet! You! You are dead!" And he slashed at Granddad, slicing him right through from side to side. Adam flinched, even though he knew that nothing could hurt Granddad now. Still it was pretty icky to watch your own grandfather fall apart into two halves and then see one of the halves start walking away from the other. But the top half quickly followed the bottom, and Granddad was soon intact again.

"I mean it literally, my dear fellow," he said to the knight. "You are dead, as in, you are not alive. Like me, you are a ghost."

"You are being ridiculous, Sirrah," the ghost said. "I have been protecting this spot for as long as I can re-member—ever since our good Queen Bess ordered me here to discover the hiding place of the mischievous rebel Queen of the Scots. The wayward infidel Mary had not yet appeared when those college miscreants came upon my hiding place and did this," he pointed at a large hole in his breastplate, "but Queen Bess said Mary would come, and wait I will until she does. Un-less . . ."

He turned his head and gave Molly a piercing look under his visor. "You are not the Scottish queen, are you, Milady? Because if you are . . ." He brandished the sword again, removing Granddad's arm.

"She is much too young to be Queen Mary," scold-ed Granddad as the arm reattached itself.

And besides, thought Molly, wasn't Mary Queen of Scots beheaded or something? Hundreds of years ago?

But the history was of less interest to Molly than the fact of that sword. It might be old but it looked really, really sharp and not ghostly at all. She suspected that the armour and the sword were all too real and that if Sir Eustace decided to go after her or Adam or her dad they would find themselves headless or armless, with no way to reattach. She was pretty sure her dad suspected the same thing because he was standing firmly in front of her and Adam; she was also pretty sure that was why Granddad was engaging the knight the way he was.

"Perhaps she is not Queen Mary," said Sir Eustace. "In which case I will not leave till the queen herself arrives! I shall never give up my post! But leave you must! Take that! And that!"

The sword zoomed through the air and through Granddad three or four times, leaving him momentarily in a number of bits and pieces, like a jigsaw puzzle. The knight paused for a moment, as he watched the puzzle remake itself. "Some kind of witchcraft must be involved. My sword never misses."

He took another swipe at Granddad, which this time went right through his neck. The blow was strong enough to send Granddad's head flying into the nearby stone wall.

"Ouch," said Granddad as his head hit the wall and then rebounded back into place again—although it first attached itself backward, and Granddad had to reach up with his hands and twist it back around.

"Ugh," said Molly.

"Double ugh," said Adam.

Sir Eustace looked at his sword as if there was something wrong with it, not something wrong with him. Or with Granddad.

Granddad tried another tack. "Look, Sir Knight or whoever you are, we are no threat to you. Our friend is locked up behind that door and as soon as we can get him out we will be out of your way."

"Ahh!" Sir Eustace answered, once more brandishing his sword. "She said you would tell me that."

"She?" asked Granddad, Molly and Adam all together.

"Yes! The poor servant lass who has been ill used—as well you know, or my name is not Sir Eustace Winslet. It's my mission to help damsels in distress—well, except for that pesky royal Scots lass Mary, of course, who deserves what she gets despite her so-called distress. But I know my damsels in distress, I do, and that serving maid is a damsel in distress if ever I saw one, right down to her tears and her very filthy apron. Ah, if I ever find the fellow who did her such a disservice, well, then he will feel the steel of my blade!"

Adam hoped that didn't also include that fellow's offspring. He backed up a little more.

Molly, meanwhile, was also backing up, and thinking about the porter upstairs, who must surely have called the police by now. So where were they and would they please, please hurry? Although once they did show up—hopefully with a key to open the door and release poor Reggie, who must be wondering what all the ruckus outside his prison was—it was going to be very awkward to try to explain about the ghostly knight.

Suddenly, the most awful thing happened. The ghost lunged right past Granddad toward their dad. Together Molly and Adam screamed, "No, no!" but to no avail. And then the ghost raised his sword, spun about, and his sword sliced right through their dad's neck.

Molly felt as though her heart had stopped. Adam too was frozen. He stopped breathing. For several seconds, nothing happened. Dad's head remained on his body, and Adam was sure that it was going to be just like in the horror movies he had seen. Slowly, ever so slowly, his dad's head would drop off his body and land with a thud on the ground. But instead his dad spoke. "That tickled."

Molly reached up and touched her dad's neck to feel for blood or a pulse or something. He turned to her and smiled. "I'm fine, Molly," he said. "That fellow really *is* a ghost. Lucinda hasn't made him real. He can't hurt us!" He laughed, and Molly thought that his laugh had a tinge of hysteria in it. And who could blame him? Almost being beheaded must be very weird, even if it only felt like a tickle.

Molly took a deep breath. "Dear Sir Knight, it is I who am the damsel in distress."

He stopped waving the sword and stared at her. "You are?"

"I am," she confirmed. Now that she had his attention, she wasn't quite sure what to do next.

The truth was probably best. "I'm afraid that Lucinda, the woman you spoke to—the maid, that is—she is . . . is . . . untrustworthy. That is, she isn't worthy of your trust."

He stared at her. "That *is* what untrustworthy means."

Great, Molly thought, sarcasm. Hasn't anyone told him that's the cheapest form of humour? She kept her thoughts to herself, however, and carried on.

"She has maligned us! She has threatened our very lives!"

"Oh dear," said the knight. "That does sound bad."

"And," Adam added, "I overheard her say that she thinks Mary would have been a better queen than Elizabeth!" It was a lie, of course—but surely it couldn't hurt.

And it didn't. The knight was furious. "She said what? How dare she! Let me at the lying wench!" The sword was flailing wildly again.

"We beg you, Sir Knight," Molly said, "to help us! Defend us!"

"Defend us from the enemy of Queen Elizabeth!" added Adam.

"We are just two poor children," Molly went on. "Albeit of good English stock."

"They are," added Granddad. "The Barnetts have been good Oxford yeomen for centuries."

"And," added Dad, "loyal subjects of their majesties!"

"And," Molly said, "that maid has imprisoned our friend! We desperately need to free him and we ask you to help us!"

Now Sir Eustace seemed uncertain.

Molly dropped to her knees and clasped her hands in a begging position. By a quick roll of her eyes, she indicated to Adam that he needed to do the same. Adam sank to his knees and then backed up Molly with all he had.

"Sir Knight," he said, "you are noble and good. We beg you to help us. We implore you! We entreat you, we plead——"

Molly jabbed Adam and hissed, "What are you? A thesaurus? Get to the point."

"Right, the point. The point is that we are two helpless children and the fellow locked up there is our . . . our . . . guardian! And without him we are not safe. And like I said, she thinks Elizabeth is a loser and Mary is wicked."

"Wicked? But you said she hated Mary."

Molly interrupted. "He means she said that Mary is wonderful, not wicked!"

"Oh," said the knight.

"So if you could just help us? Please?" added Molly.

The knight hesitated.

"And," Dad threw in, "Lucinda also said that Mary was prettier than Elizabeth, by far."

"And," added Adam, "was better at . . . at . . ." He couldn't think of anything.

"At trigonometry," Molly said. It was the first thing that popped into her head.

"It's a lie!" Sir Eustace said. "A gross calumny! Elizabeth is the best mathematician amongst the crowned heads of Europe! I'll have the wench's guts for garters!" Then he suddenly turned and stared at Molly again. "But how do I know *you* are not lying to me?

"Stop!" a voice came from the gloom behind them. "Stop in the name of the law!"

The police had finally arrived.

As two policemen hurried down the corridor with the porter following behind, the beams of their flashlights pierced through the gloom, shining on the Barnetts and forcing Molly and Adam to close their eyes. As they reopened them, Granddad blinked out of sight—and so did Sir Eustace.

Adam wondered why Sir Eustace disappeared. The knight must be used to disappearing when people visited the crypt, otherwise he'd be the most famous ghost in the history of the world. But then why had he appeared to Adam and Molly and Dad just now? Had

Lucinda arranged it somehow, or were they all just getting better at seeing ghosts?

"Here they are, officers," said the man from the gate. "Just as I told you."

"You're trespassing here," said one of the policeman. "We're going to have to ask you to leave."

"But officer," said Dad, "there's a man locked up here."

"Behind this door," added Molly. "Can't you hear him?"

And indeed, there were muffled shouts coming from behind the door.

"Oh, dear," said the porter. He pulled out a huge ring of keys, muttering to himself as he searched for the right one. "I don't know how he managed to get down here! I certainly never let anyone pass. Perhaps Cedric? He was on duty last night. Or perhaps one of the students . . . Ah, here it is!"

He inserted the key in a lock, and in a flash, the door opened and Reggie strode out. He wore a purple shirt decorated with white flowers and there was an empty water bottle in his hand. Before he even said hello he held up his left hand and showed them the ring.

"She didn't get it off me!" he said triumphantly.

CHAPTER TEN

Hunting for Sustenance

It took a long time to explain everything in a way that satisfied both the porter and the policemen. Assisted by Molly and Adam, Reggie came up with a story about how he was a tourist who had wandered in to take a look at the college and somehow found his way down into the crypt, where he'd taken a few photos with his phone when suddenly the door slammed shut and he found himself locked up.

"I promise you," he told the porter, "I just walked in—there wasn't anybody there to stop me."

"But it's impossible," the porter replied. "I've been at the gate all day, ever since I came on duty at seven."

"Don't you take a lunch break?" said Molly.

The porter was very offended. "I bring my lunch, I never leave my post!"

"Not even to go to the bathroom?" asked Adam curiously.

"Well," the porter admitted, his face turning a bit red, "there was one quick trip to the loo."

"It could happen to anyone," said Dad sympathetically. "At any rate, thank you for your help."

"Well," said the porter, "I'm sorry I didn't believe you sooner, but, like they say, Sir, rules is rules."

The four of them finally made their way up out of the darkness and toward the bright sunshine. The knight had not reappeared—and neither had Granddad.

It was a lovely spring day, something Molly hadn't appreciated until forced to spend time in the dank, dark cellar. And it made her very tired, because it reminded her that back home it was still night and the sun probably hadn't even come up yet. She'd slept a little on the plane, but not much, and she found herself yawning. Jet lag was a terrible thing.

"By the way," said Adam, "just how did you get down there, Reggie? I mean, how did Lucinda get you past the guard?"

"That's an excellent question, Adam," his dad said, "But there are a lot of other questions we have to ask Reggie—equally excellent ones. And I, for one, am feeling very hungry. How about the rest of you?"

"I could certainly use a bite or two," said Reggie.

"Me, too, I guess," said Molly, who was actually thinking that a hot bath and ten or fifteen hours of sleep would be much better.

"Do you have to ask?" said Adam. For him, the sandwiches he'd eaten a few hours earlier were just a distant memory.

"So let's eat and save the questions until then," Dad decided.

"Where?" asked Adam, as he looked around hopefully for a nearby hamburger joint.

"We could go back to the cottage," said Dad.

"In Toot Baldon," Molly said.

"Yes," said Adam, "Toot Baldon."

Dad ignored them. "We could pick up your mom," he continued, "and go out for dinner. Or we could just eat there—I think she got enough food for dinner, too."

"Let's leave it up to her, Dad," said Molly, who just wanted a nice soft bed.

They headed for the car, but when they got to where they'd parked it, it was nowhere in sight.

"Lucinda strikes again," said Dad.

"Er, I don't think so, Dad," said Adam. "Look at the road." He pointed at the place where the car had been. There were double yellow lines painted on the pavement. "Those lines mean there's no parking there, right? Not ever. I bet the car has been towed away by the police."

Adam remembered the two yellow lines from earlier visits—his dad had a very bad habit of pretending not to notice them, often with very bad results.

His dad made use of some of his extensive vocabulary. "It's bad enough when an evil ghost plays tricks on you, but it's even worse when the police end up helping her. What do we do now?"

"I had a car, remember?" Reggie said. "And unless Lucinda's made off with it—which I doubt—I know just where it is. This way."

He began to stride purposefully down the street and around the corner. Everyone followed along behind him.

"Voila!" Reggie said, pointing to a very small red car. "I made sure it was parked legally, even though Lucinda tried to get me to go closer to the college. Told her she didn't want to make herself too interesting to the authorities."

Reggie was nothing if not bossy, thought Adam. Even in the midst of being kidnapped, he was giving instructions to the kidnapper on how to do it properly.

"With a bit of luck," Reggie added, "we might all fit in."

It would have to be luck. To Adam, the little car didn't even seem big enough to fit Reggie.

But in fact they did all manage to squeeze in; Adam and Molly with their heads bumping in the truly teeny back seat and Dad up front beside Reggie. In a few minutes they were far from the colleges and on their way out of Oxford.

They arrived back at the cottage to find a very

upset Mom.

"Reggie!" she said. "Thank heavens you're here and safe!" She looked at their dad and said, "I did not enjoy being stuck here unable to help."

Molly thought that was probably an understatement. Mom always had to be the one in charge, the one who was doing. Being out at the cottage with no car and no way to help must have driven her half crazy!

In order to give her mom something else to think about, Molly brought up how hungry they all were. They decided to drive back into Oxford for dinner.

With Mom in the car—Molly was sort of half sitting on her knees and sort of leaning on Adam, who was mashed up against the window—the first part of the drive was even tighter and squishier than before. Fortunately, it was a short drive. Reggie had got on his phone and learned that the place they kept the impounded cars was not far away, in a lot beside the gasometer on the road into town. After getting a mercifully brief lecture from the attendant about being a scofflaw, and handing over an amazingly thick wad of pound notes— they did take parking very seriously in Oxford—Dad found himself back in the driver's seat of their rented car. He and Mom and Molly followed Reggie and Adam as they searched for a restaurant.

"There's a good place down that street just up there," said Granddad, suddenly popping into view in the backseat of Reggie's car.

"Turn left here, Reggie."

"Yes, Sir," said Reggie, making the turn, and looking back to make sure the other car followed.

"Look for Carrington and Sons," said Granddad. "They have these really wonderful bloater paste sandwiches."

"Bloater paste?" said Adam. "What's that?" And could anything with a name that had bloat in it possibly taste good?

"It's a kind of fish, actually," said Granddad. "Although, it's really more suitable for lunch than dinner. For dinner, you'll probably want to order something more substantial, like steak and kidney pie or bangers and mash."

Kidney? Wasn't that something disgusting from inside your body? And what could a banger be? After mistakenly tasting headcheese, Adam wasn't the least bit sure that he wanted to find out.

Fortunately, he didn't have to. When they got to the place where Granddad said the restaurant would be, there was no sign for Carrington and Sons. Instead, the sign said Pizza Scholars.

"Where did that come from?" Granddad asked. "I could swear it wasn't there last month."

As Adam once more gently reminded Granddad that the last month he was remembering was many years ago, the others pulled up behind and got out of the car.

"Are we really going to have pizza?" asked Mom. "I was kind of looking forward to something more, well, British."

"Like bangers?" said Adam

"Perhaps," said Mom, "or maybe a delicious dish of braised sweetbreads."

"Mmm, sweetbreads," said Dad. "Been yonks since I had some. It's a cow's pancreas, you know," he told Adam.

Could it possibly be that Adam's parents were teasing him? Well, he didn't care, there was no way he was going to eat a pancreas, and that was that.

"I'm voting for pizza," he said firmly.

"And I'm soooooo tired," said Molly, who was too sleepy to care about food at all. "And we're here now. Let's go in." She began to march toward the door, with Adam following right behind.

Her mom and dad, laughing a little, came too.

"I suppose a pizza wouldn't hurt," said Dad.

"And I can always get my sweetbreads another day, now that we're here in England," said Mom. Adam turned and gave her a very dark look. How could she tease him about food, of all things? Food was a serious matter. He breathed deeply, and then relaxed. Pizza—it smelled like good old North American pizza: tomatoes, pepperoni, cheese—nothing English about it. And, as far as he could tell, no headcheese anywhere.

Within moments, they were seated at a table in a dark corner. Mom asked for an extra chair for someone who hadn't arrived yet, and then Granddad hovered over it. They weren't certain about whether or not he was visible to the other customers, but it hardly mattered——the restaurant was dimly lit and so busy it'd be surprising if anyone even noticed him, let alone worried about whether or not he was actually there. And he needed to be part of the conversation.

"Are you ready to order?" a young man asked. Dad and Mom decided to share a large pepperoni, and after saying she wasn't hungry and having her mother tell her she needed to eat, Molly settled on a small vegetarian.

Much to Adam's surprise, Reggie said he thought that sounded good, and ordered the same thing. How could he be so large if he ate so little? After trying to decide between a Mexican pizza and a Hawaiian, Adam settled on a combination of the two——ground beef, ham, bacon, onion, green peppers, hot peppers, refried beans, avocado, maraschino cherries, olives, pineapple, sour cream, and three kinds of cheese. His mouth watered in anticipation.

"And you, Sir?" the waiter asked Granddad. "What would you like?"

CHAPTER ELEVEN
A Side Order of Haunting

For a moment there was silence as everyone realized that Granddad was visible after all. Adam hoped the waiter wouldn't notice that Granddad wasn't exactly sitting on his chair, but hovering slightly over it.

"You don't have any steak-and-kidney pie, do you?" Granddad finally said.

"Our specialty," said the waiter. "The Pizza Scholars' British pizza: steak, kidney, bangers, bloater, brawn—which I believe you Yanks call headcheese—and of course, tomato sauce and cheese."

"Uh, yes, I'll have that," said Granddad.

The waiter nodded and left. Adam figured it was too dark for him to see that Granddad wasn't quite your normal patron.

"Tomatoes and cheese," said Granddad. "What's the world coming to? Oh well, it's not as if I'm actually going to be able to eat it," he added. "I just wanted to look at it for a bit."

Adam was glad that he wasn't sitting beside Granddad. Just the thought of headcheese made his stomach turn over.

As they waited for their food, Reggie told them about his encounter with Lucinda.

"She is quite a piece of work," he said. "I was driving here to meet up with you folks when she stopped me."

"Yes," said Adam, "Granddad told us."

"She materialized inside the car, told me to stop, which I did since I was afraid she might grab the wheel or something, and then she demanded the ring. But I refused to give it to her. I said I'd rather die. Before I even realized what she was doing, she tried to pull the ring off my finger—and she couldn't. It was like there was some . . . some force or something stopping her. Almost like the ring didn't want her to have it."

"Interesting," mused Granddad. "Very interesting."

"Anyway, that made her even angrier. She said that if she couldn't get the ring herself, then I was going to have to give it to her. When I said I wouldn't, well, she did this . . . well, this thing."

"Thing?" said Dad. "What thing?"

"I was sitting there in the car looking out at the highway," said Reggie, "and suddenly, the highway wasn't there. Instead, I was seeing my brother Len—you remember my twin Lennie, from Palm Springs?"

"Yes, of course," said Dad.

"Well, he was floating there, somehow, in midair, on the other side of the windshield, and looking very frightened. And I also could see why he was frightened—he was standing on a railing at the very top of a high building, and there was a fellow behind him getting ready to push him over. It was a vision of some sort, you see? And Lucinda said that if I didn't get the car going and take her where she wanted us to go, she'd order that man to push Lennie off the building."

"Good grief!" said Molly. Well, what could you expect from someone willing to destroy the world.

"So I decided I had to do as she said," Reggie added.

"A good thing, too," said Granddad. "The woman is ruthless. Your brother was not safe, not safe at all."

Reggie nodded. "I'm just hoping that poor Len wasn't really on top of a building—he's almost as afraid of heights as he is of being on an airplane. I've been trying to get hold of him, but with no luck so far. At any rate, I drove her into Oxford and let her lead me into that old college."

"It's actually New College," said Granddad.

"It sure didn't look new," said Reggie.

"Wasn't there a porter there to stop you?" Granddad asked.

"I suppose he might have stopped us," said Reggie, "if he hadn't been sound asleep. Anyway, I refused to go down the stairs, so she pushed me down! And then she had this knight there who threatened me with a sword. I didn't know if he was 'materialized' like her or not. And she seems to be able to go back and forth between having a real body and being a ghost—after all she must have travelled out there to the highway as a ghost and then materialized."

"Sir Eustace," interrupted Adam. "That's the name of that knight. And he didn't have a body. Not so far, anyway."

"I wish I'd known that," said Reggie. "But I couldn't take the chance, so there I was—stuck until I agreed to give her the ring. Her plan was simple: she couldn't overpower me so she would wait until I slept or starved and get it from me one way or the other."

"What I'm wondering," said Adam, "is who the man was that she had helping her. The man you saw with Lennie, I mean. Another ghost?"

"If he was going to push a living person off a building," said Molly, "he couldn't be a ghost. Not anymore."

"Which means," said Mom, "that she may have already begun to gather a gang of re-bodied ghosts around her. Ghosts with no shred of goodness in them."

"Come to think of it," said Reggie, "I did think that man behind Lennie in the vision looked familiar. He had this huge moustache, and a sort of iron hat. It's weird, but when I looked at him, I found myself thinking of Kaiser Wilhelm, who was the emperor of Germany in World War I. I once read a book about him."

"I've read about him too," said Dad. "Kaiser Wilhelm was a little nutty, as well as being ruthless and responsible for thousands of deaths. He'd be just the kind of man Lucinda could use for her own purposes. We're going to have to act fast."

The waiter arrived with their food, and soon they were all digging in to their pizzas, even Molly. The scary conversation had woken her up despite her jet lag, and she found she was hungrier than she'd thought. She might even have to beg Adam for a slice of his pizza, which looked both disgusting and, strangely, appetizing.

Adam, meanwhile, was inhaling slices as fast as could. The Mexi-Hawaiian was a great idea. Who knew refried beans would go so well with pineapple? It tasted so good he was hardly even aware of the noxious smells of kidney and bloater coming from Granddad's pizza sitting on the other side of the table.

Granddad was staring longingly at his food. "Kidney," he said. "There actually is kidney on it. It's been so long since I've had kidney. So very long. If I could have just one bite. . . ."

Oh no! Surely Granddad wasn't thinking of returning to his body just for a bite of pizza!

"Don't do it, Granddad!" Adam said. "Much as we'd like to have you alive again, you're more useful as a ghost."

"I know," said Granddad, wistfully. "I wouldn't really do it—not for a taste of kidney, at any rate. But it does smell good. Could somebody move it to the other side of the table?"

Mom picked it up and handed it to Reggie, who made a face as he smelled it and then put it down beside his own plate.

As Adam ate, he found himself worrying over Reggie's story. Something about it was bothering him.

Well, it was unsettling, and that was for sure. As usual, Lucinda seemed to have pretty much taken leave of her senses. And now she had at least one other madman on her side, some guy in an iron hat who apparently liked to kill people. There was also a good chance that that knight with the sword down in the dungeon was on his way back toward a real body too. Lucinda did seem to have a thing about men wearing metal. He shuddered to think about how she'd respond if she met some dead biker gang with a lot of piercings and hobnailed boots. Make them her private army or something.

The fact that of the three things they needed—the ring, the necklace, and the elephant—they still had only the ring, and had almost lost that, was also pretty upsetting. And the fact that they hadn't found the necklace yet. And the fact that Lucinda now had the elephant, as far as they could tell. And who knew, maybe she had the necklace too! Anything was possible. All that was standing between the world and sure destruction was Reggie and the ring on his finger. How were they going to keep him safe? Should they do something else with the ring?

"I'm wondering," said his mom between bites of pizza, "shouldn't we be doing something else with that ring? I mean, is it safe for Reggie to keep it on?"

"Just what I was thinking," said Adam.

"From what Reggie has told us," said Granddad, "I think his finger is the safest place of all."

"It does seem," said Dad, "that Lucinda can't get her hands on it while it's there."

"I wonder why," said Adam. "It must have something to do with that curse. That poem: 'The living undone.' Hmm." He was soon lost in thought.

"There you go again with that stupid poem," said Molly crossly. The food was making her tired again. "Anyway, maybe Reggie's finger *is* the best place," she continued, "but then I think he needs to be guarded at all times. What do you say, Granddad? Don't you think you should stick with Reggie from now on? I mean, we just can't let Lucinda get her hands on him again, and a ghost has a better chance of guarding him than anyone else."

"Yes, I agree," said Granddad with a sigh. "Another reason for me not to eat those kidneys. And I've brought some friends along to help me guard him. You remember Shorty and Bart?"

Adam remembered the two ghosts they had met in The Living Desert near Palm Springs. One was a grizzly gold miner, the other a skeleton. In fact, there was a skeleton standing in the restaurant right now, on the other side of the table from Adam.

"Howdy, folks," he said. "Is that kidneys I'm smellin'? I always did have a likin' fer kidneys—back when I had my own innards, I mean."

"Not now, Bart!" Granddad shouted. "Go! Vamoose! Scat!"

Bart nodded and then blinked out of view. Fortunately, he'd come and gone so quickly that no one else in the restaurant seemed to have noticed.

"Sorry about that," said Granddad. "But you have to admit, the kidneys do smell fine. I myself will be much happier far away from them—and so, I guess, will Bart. So you folks finish your meal, and I'll take Bart and Shorty back to The Oaks and wait for you there. You can bring Reggie home with you, and Bart, Shorty, and I will wait with him while the rest of you try to find the pendant."

"All right," said Mom. "But should you leave us now?"

"I think it'll be okay, Lily," Granddad reassured her. "Even Lucinda isn't brazen enough to suddenly show up in a crowded restaurant."

"Oh, yes I am," said Lucinda, who had, indeed, suddenly shown up, looking very out of place in her old-fashioned maid's uniform.

Uh oh, thought Adam, Lucinda had obviously become pretty good at changing back and forth between being a ghost and being in her body. That was not good news. It probably meant that Granddad could change back and forth just like Lucinda, but at what cost? Maybe going back and forth between being a ghost and not being a ghost was what was making Lucinda so totally mental.

As if to prove his point, Lucinda began to laugh—a crazy laugh, so loud that everyone in the restaurant turned and stared.

"Madam," said the waiter as he hurried over. "Are you all right? Would you like a drink of water?"

"Water? No. I don't need water. I need eyes! A green one and a blue one. Right now I'll settle for a green one. And you, Mr. Crankshaft," she turned to Reggie with a vicious smile, "you might as well just hand it over now and be done with it. Because I want you to know that I'll stop at nothing. You might not fear for your own safety, but there are others here that I can hurt." She laughed again. "I can hurt them badly."

Molly shuddered. Who might she hurt? And how? And when?

"Go away, Lucinda," said Granddad. "This is neither the time nor the place."

"Yeah, git," said Bart, as he appeared beside her.

"Vamoose," added Shorty from the other side, the knife stuck permanently into his chest wiggling wildly back and forth.

"All right," she said calmly. "I will go—for now. Maybe. Or maybe I won't. Maybe I'll just stay here invisibly. I can do that, too, you know. Stay here and listen to your every word, your every plan. Yes!" she crowed. "You'll never keep any secrets from me! Because I can always be there, listening, and I can always be one step ahead of you!"

She laughed again and then blinked out as quickly as she had appeared, followed by Shorty and Bart.

For a while nobody did or said anything. The entire restaurant was silent as everyone stared at the place where, they were all convinced, a woman in a maid's uniform had just been standing—and was that, could it have been, some sort of talking skeleton? Finally, the waiter spoke.

"Do . . . do you know that lady?" he finally asked. "And those . . . those . . ."

"Never saw her in my life," said Dad in a firm voice. "Must be some kind of actor or something. Or an initiation, maybe. I didn't realize you had these sorts of problems here in Oxford."

"Yes," added Mom, "you really do need to think about better security. It's quite put me off my pizza."

"Me, too," said Molly, as she saw what they were trying to do.

"Uh, me, too," said Adam, who nevertheless had just taken another big bite.

"Please bring the bill," Mom added icily.

"Uh, yes, Ma'am, of course," the waiter said. "And I'll talk to the manager about that . . . that actor. Right now. And those . . . those . . ."

And he backed off looking very confused, as the restaurant began to fill up with noise—everyone was talking about what they'd just seen and trying to figure it out. Molly had no doubt that people with phones had been clicking photos and that the whole episode would end up on YouTube in moments. It would probably be reported on the BBC as another strange incident.

"Lucinda is indeed becoming more brazen," said Granddad grimly. "We're going to have to be very, very careful."

Especially, thought Molly, if she does what she'd just said she'd do. She could be here, there, every-where, in her body and out of it at will, it seemed. Even if they did discover where Lucinda had hidden the elephant, how would they get it back from her? And how would they keep her from finding out what they were up to? How would they even manage to get Reggie back to Toot Baldon without Lucinda knowing their every move?

That's when Molly had an idea. It was a completely logical thing and Molly was always logical. She took out her little writing pad from her purse and wrote a small note on it, keeping her hand over the page so no one could see it; even if there was a ghost leaning over her shoulder, she wouldn't be able to read it. Molly then folded it and passed it to Adam, who knew what the ghost was doing and read it still mostly folded so no one could see.

"If we split up, she can't follow all of us at once," Molly had written. Adam nodded in agreement, then passed the note on to his dad, who read it, nodded, winked at Molly in approval, passed it on to Molly's mom, and finally to Reggie.

Mom said, "I think we all agree with Molly. But for now it's late, it's been a long day and everyone must be exhausted. We are going back to the cottage to sleep and in the morning we'll each have a job to do."

And after the waiter came with the bill, Mom paid it, and they headed off to do just that.

CHAPTER TWELVE
Treasure Hunt

"**M**olly! Get up! Now!"

Somehow, Molly had slept as if she hadn't a worry in the world, even though by the time she finally got into bed, it was just the middle of the afternoon back home. She would have kept right on sleeping, too, if her annoying brother hadn't screamed in her ear that it was time to get up.

Well, he was right, of course. They did have to save the world. But who could save the world without enough sleep? And her hair must be a total mess; she'd have to deal with that first. Once she was actually ready to get up. She rolled over and hoped for just a few minutes more.

Well, so much for that, thought Adam as he stared down at his sister, who was already sound asleep again. When Molly was like that, even a piledriver in the next room couldn't wake her. Sighing, he headed down to the kitchen.

Adam himself had been nothing but glad when morning finally arrived and he could get up and start the day. He had spent the night tossing and turning in the twin bed beside Molly, who was annoyingly dead to the world. It felt like he hadn't slept at all—but he must have, because he woke up remembering horrible dreams about knights with shining blades that sliced through flesh, about ghostly children who had died in their beds from strange maladies, and about platoons of wasps in black uniforms and dirty aprons, whose heads turned into big wedges of bright orange cheese. And whatever it was, it always finally turned into Lucinda, Lucinda with her crazy laugh and her total and complete insanity. How do you battle with someone who's beyond help?

And then, after it was already a little light outside and he finally did really fall sound asleep, he suddenly awoke with a start, the words of that poem repeating again and again: "And chaos shall come / And the loud shall be dumb / And the living undone."

It meant something. Something important. He just knew it. If only he could figure out what.

Which he couldn't.

Reggie was already in the kitchen cooking what he called a "full English," which consisted of eggs, bacon, toast, sausage, baked beans, jam, marmalade, and orange juice.

And bloater paste.

Well, the sausage and beans and jam and all looked pretty good, Adam told himself. He could just avoid the bloater paste.

As Reggie's hands flashed here and there, stirring things and moving pans, Adam couldn't help but notice that Reggie was still wearing the emerald ring. It probably was the best idea. But it seemed so foolhardy somehow, with the world on the verge of extinction— almost as if Reggie were flaunting the ring, daring Lucinda to come and get it.

And who knew, maybe she was already here, invisible, trying some ghostly trick to make it slither off Reggie's finger.

It was very scary. And it made Adam very hungry.

"Can I help?" Adam asked Reggie.

"No help needed," Reggie replied. "You just sit down there like a good little boy and wait. It'll take no time at all."

But it was obvious to Adam that it was going to take much too much time. Sighing yet again, he decided that he might as well go outside and get some fresh air. It would certainly be better than hanging around in the kitchen surrounded by delicious smells and unable to eat anything.

First, though, and after checking to make sure Reggie was too busy at the stovetop to notice, he found

the giant economy-sized box of Jaffa Cakes his mom
had got at Tesco's yesterday, and grabbed three. Adam
loved the delicious orangey and chocolatey biscuits,
and you couldn't get them back home, so his parents
always made sure there was a good supply on hand
when they came to England. Adam hadn't had a Jaffa
Cake for years now, not since Gram died. And it would
help him to wait for breakfast.

He grabbed his jacket, put it on, stuffed two of the
biscuits into the pockets, shoved one into his mouth,
and headed outside. His first thought was the little
glade with the tree house. John might be there. He felt
bad for the poor kid, just finding out that he was dead
and everything. He wondered how he was doing.

But would it be a good idea to go there? What if
Lucinda was on guard, just waiting for Adam to do
something stupid? What if she found out about John
and did something awful to scare him? John was a Barnett, after all, and she sure did seem to have a thing
about Barnetts.

But wasn't Lucinda more likely to be hanging around
the kitchen, keeping her eye on Reggie and that ring?
Wouldn't that be more important to her? After all, he
himself was just a kid, and so was John. How could
either of them possibly matter to her? He headed over
to the glade.

Nobody was there. The dew was still on the grass,
so he didn't want to sit and wait, and calling out to

John might attract the wrong sort of attention. He leaned against the tree, devoured the other two cakes and then, figuring breakfast must be about ready, turned to head back to the house. A strange sound stopped him in his tracks. Was it birds singing? No, it sounded more like laughter—but very far away. Could it be Lucinda again?

"Hello, Adam," said a cheerful voice.

John! As Adam turned to see the little boy, the laughter got closer and louder. John had appeared at the worse possible time!

"I have a friend," said John cheerfully.

"John," Adam cried, "you shouldn't be here. It's too dangerous right now!"

"Don't be silly," said John. "It's just the garden behind the house. How can it be dangerous? As long as you don't try to climb the trees, of course. And I promised my momma I wouldn't climb any trees, and I haven't, and I won't—except for the ladder up to the tree house. So there!"

"But you don't understand," said Adam, very frightened now. "It's not the trees, it's—."

"I told my new friend about not climbing the trees," John continued, "and she said momma was right. So I'm not going to do it ever. Not until I'm old enough."

Wait a minute, Adam told himself. This friend of John's—it was a she? And was that still the strange laughter, coming yet nearer? Could it be . . . ?

"John," said Adam slowly, "who is this new friend? It isn't a lady in a black dress is it?"

"No, of course not," said John. "She has a white dress on."

So maybe it wasn't Lucinda? But Lucinda could always change her dress, couldn't she? The old one was certainly in need of a good wash.

"At first," added John, "I thought she was an angel. But she didn't have any wings, and then I noticed that she has a bunch of medals. Like a soldier! A lady soldier!"

But not, Adam, hoped, a rifle. Or a sword.

"We play soldiers sometimes," said John.

That didn't sound good.

"So I'm glad she's not an angel. But Adam," John's voice was very serious now, "I have to say sorry to you."

"To me? Why?"

"Because . . . because you were right. About me, I mean. I am dead. My friend told me it was true. She says I'm the one who's an angel! Not the kind with wings, though," John said a little sadly. "Wings would be fun! But it must have been terrible for Momma. When I died, I mean. Poor Momma."

"I'm sure it was," Adam told him, "but, well, now she'll be . . . uh . . . at peace too." Then a new thought struck Adam. "Have you met her? I mean, she should be on the other side, too, right?"

John was already pale, but he seemed to pale more. "You mean . . . my momma is . . . is dead?" Tears began to appear in the corners of his eyes.

Oh, great. Adam could have kicked himself. He'd just been trying to help. And now the laughter was there again, louder—and it seemed to be laughing at him for being such a stupid jerk.

"Yes," he said, "She is, John. I'm so sorry, I really am. But it was a long time ago, you know. I mean, it's new to you, but—" Then a new thought struck him. "I wonder why she hasn't found you, or why you couldn't find her . . . ?"

"I can answer that," said a voice that was very familiar. And standing there, right beside John, was Reggie.

Reggie in a white dress. With a row of medals across the chest.

"Reggie?" Adam said. He had no problem with Reggie dressing in girl's clothes. He had a friend in school who liked to do that—Garrin Kozlik. Garrin sometimes even wore eye shadow; it was just Garrin being Garrin. But wasn't Reggie in the kitchen right now, wearing yet another loud shirt, this one with crocodiles and hula dancers on it? How could he have changed clothes and gotten out here so fast?

"Yes," said Reggie in his usual loud, booming voice. "Reggie it is! How did you know my nickname?"

"But Reggie," said Adam, confused, "of course I know your name. I mean—"

129

"Nonsense," Reggie interrupted. "We've never met before. But I guess the lad must have told you, eh, Johnny boy? Anyway, I'm pleased to meet you."

Reggie reached out and tried to shake Adam's hand.

Oh my gosh, thought Adam, as the hand went right through his. Reggie is a ghost after all! We always did think there was something fishy about him. I mean, the way he got out of those ropes at the lake and all. And maybe his being in that dungeon was all a trick! Maybe he's actually on Lucinda's side! Maybe—

"Drat," said Reggie, taking a close look at the hand. "I'm always doing that. It's so hard to remember you're dead sometimes. At any rate, I'm Regina Crankshaft."

Regina Crankshaft! Of course! Adam suddenly remembered the old newspaper clipping he and Molly had found in Granddad's desk last summer, with a photograph of a woman who looked just like Reggie, but wearing a nurse's uniform.

A uniform just like the one this woman was wearing.

Regina Crankshaft really was a woman, and not the Reggie that Adam knew at all. She was an ancestor of their Reggie. It was all coming back to him now. She'd served in some war back in the old days, and before that she'd been a nurse for his great-great-grandfather Maurice when he died.

One way or the other, she, too, had died and now, here she was, back again. Why?

"I've been taking care of the lad, sort of watching over him," she explained. "To be perfectly honest, you know, I'm not completely sure why I'm doing it; I never did like the little ones all that much. Never had any of my own, either. But somehow . . ." She looked a little bewildered.

Somehow, Adam told himself, she couldn't help herself. Yet again, like Reggie and Lennie, like that Fitzie Crankshaft who tried to get the eyes back into the elephant in the very old days, like the Crankshaft who helped Adam's granddad's dad in the war. It seemed that Crankshafts were always looking out for the Barnetts.

"I wonder if I should be telling you all this," Regina added. "You're a perfect stranger, after all. That's why I was trying to frighten you away with my scary laugh."

She proceeded to produce the laugh that Adam had assumed was Lucinda. "It is very scary, isn't it?"

"Yes," said Adam, "it is."

Even now, when he knew she was just doing it as a demonstration, it sent chills up his spine.

"It's actually an imitation of an African spotted hyena—*Crocuta crocuta*, you know. It's the call it makes to escape attackers. I learned it during my time out there in the Boer War. I'm glad it scared you, even though I don't actually seem to be worried about you now that I've met you. Somehow, in fact, I'm absolutely convinced the boy is your friend. And . . ." She seemed puzzled. "And," she finally added, "I feel compelled to look after *you*, too. You don't happen to need a bath or a bowl of gruel, do you?"

"Uh, no, no, I'm fine."

"I wonder," she said. "You look a little peaked."

"It's just jet lag," said Adam.

"Jet what?"

"Never mind. Anyway, it's him we should be worried about." Adam pointed toward John, who was smiling up at them happily. "The thing is, well, I'm wondering if you might be able to help John find his mother."

"Oh, yes, please," said John.

"I would if I knew who she was," Regina said. "But he doesn't remember his momma's name. And if little master John's momma isn't here, then she must have crossed over. She must have thought he was there already, and didn't know he was stuck. Until now, I had no idea about how to help him get across and join her. But now you're here, I believe it can be done. I intend to help him cross over, with your assistance."

"Me?"

"Yes, you see, we who are still here can't cross over as long as there is something unfinished in our lives. I myself . . ." She paused, and her face turned red. "Well, we won't go into that just now. But little John here—he can't cross while he's still pulled to this spot. He did something that he needs to put right, you see."

"What's that?" Adam asked. This was getting more and more interesting.

"He buried something in the ground. It was just a small boy's prank, nothing of great significance in the larger scheme of things. But it preys on the poor lad's mind."

"I was going to put it back," John said. "It was part of a pretend game I was playing with my friend Cecil. We were pirates, you see, and we were burying treasure and then we had to find the treasure—that is, he had to find mine and I had to find his. But then I got so, so sick and I couldn't go outside and play with Cecil anymore. And then, I guess, I died, and we never did get to finish the game. And I felt so terrible because Momma really loved that pendant and I know I shouldn't have taken it in the first place, but it was so bright and shiny, just like real pirate's treasure. And oh, dear, Momma must have been very, very sad when she couldn't find it." John began to sniffle as Regina tried to pat him on his back.

"There, there," she said.

For a moment Adam thought he must have heard wrong.

"Did you say pendant?" he finally asked.

"Yes," said John. "It was Momma's favourite. The jewel was so very, very blue. Poppa said it was just the colour of her eyes."

"And," said Adam, "you buried it over there by the tree? Where you were trying to dig before?"

"Yes," said John, giggling a little. "That's where the treasure trove lies, me matey. By yon sturdy oak."

"I believe that's a beech tree, actually," said Regina. "You can tell by the sparsely toothed leaves. *Sylvatica*, you know—it's one of the *Fagaceae*. But what I'm thinking is that you"—she pointed at Adam—"are still alive. Although much too pale. A calming clover tea might help, and a diet of groats and headcheese. Anyway, you can dig it up and, maybe return it to the rightful owner, if you can figure out who that is."

"I believe it might actually be me," said Adam. "Or at least my family. I think John here is related to me—a great-great-uncle or something like that."

"Fancy that," said Regina. "Well then," she added briskly, "that makes it much easier. You dig up the pendant, and then, I suspect, John can finally cross over and be at peace."

Adam didn't need to be told twice.

First, he had John show him exactly where to dig. Then he asked Regina, "Could you, please, just go wherever you go when you aren't here? I mean, is there a way to see if there are any other ghosts about?"

He didn't want to show Lucinda where the pendant was.

"I suppose," she said. "May I ask why?"

There didn't seem to be any harm in telling her, so Adam gave Regina a brief explanation of the events that had brought him and his family to England, and the entire world to the brink of destruction.

"My goodness," she said. "That is quite a story. And you say you know another Reggie Crankshaft? Interesting, very interesting. Yes, of course, I'll go take a gander on the astral plane for you."

Regina blinked out—and then, almost immediately, blinked back in again. "Nobody's there," she said. "You may proceed."

Nodding, Adam kneeled down and began to dig, John beside him and thrusting his hands through the ground to no effect and singing, "Sixteen men on a dead man's chest, Yo ho ho and a bottle of rum."

At first the ground was quite hard—it hadn't been disturbed for more than a hundred years—but surprisingly soon, Adam's hand felt something. After a bit more digging, he pulled on a thick chain and slowly uncovered a pendant. He brushed the dirt off it until he could see that it was a long gold chain. Attached to it was a blue stone, set inside a gold casing.

The sapphire! The Morning Eye!

"That's it!" said John with a squeal of delight. "The

pirate treasure! Momma's pendant! Oh, thank you, thank you, thank you, Adam. You are my bestest friend!"

Alarmed, Adam shushed John, and tried not to think about what he held in his hand. He had no idea if Lucinda was near enough to listen.

"I suggest," said Regina, "That we call it something else. Let's call it—I don't know—the icebox."

"Oh," said John. "What fun! Adam has dug up Momma's icebox." He giggled again.

"Yes, indeed, dear," said Regina, "he has. And now, he'll need to consult with his family about who to give the icebox to. Right, Adam?"

"Oh," said Adam. "The icebox. My family. Right."

"Now dear," Regina said to John, "let's let him do what he has to do—and maybe, just maybe, you'll be able to see your momma soon."

"Oh! I hope so!" And with that the two of them were gone.

Adam nervously pushed the pend—no, the icebox—into his jacket pocket, not wanting Lucinda or any other passing ghost to get a glimpse. But he couldn't stop himself from being overjoyed. He had what they needed so badly!

He grinned. Molly was never going to believe this.

Then the grin left his face.

How was he even going to tell her without Lucinda finding out? He looked around nervously. Could she already know? Regina had said she wasn't near, but might the unearthing of the Morning Eye somehow have attracted her?

No, not the Mor—the thing. The icebox.

Feeling an unsettling mixture of happiness and fear, Adam headed toward the house.

CHAPTER THIRTEEN
Another Hunt for the Hidden

W hen Adam walked into the cottage, his dad had his cell in his hand—checking his emails and looking at the news headlines, probably.

"It's getting worse all the time," Dad was telling Molly. "Now it looks like it's spreading everywhere. Some kid who insisted on being called Billy got arrested in New Mexico for trying to shoot up a herd of cattle—said the ranch they were on was actually his."

"A kid?" said Molly. "Billy? Oh, I get it. Billy the Kid!"

"Right—a mean dude if there ever was one. And in Chicago, a Mr. Capone and three accomplices held up a liquor store with machine guns and accused the owner of ruining their business. And wait, here's another: an old guy with a beard broke into the Parliament buildings in Ottawa and tried to make a speech about something called reciprocity in a thick Scottish accent, all the while taking swigs out of a bottle of whiskey."

"Reciprocity . . . John A. Macdonald, right? The first prime minister?" Molly knew she shouldn't be having fun with this, but it was almost like playing on a game show—and so far she'd guessed them all correctly.

Dad nodded. "And a man dressed in nothing but a sheet tried to buy an elephant from a travelling circus in Switzerland, saying he needed it for a trip across the Alps."

"Weird," said Molly. "You can't take an elephant across a mountain range."

"It has been done," said Reggie, "by a famous and very tough-minded enemy of the ancient Romans. Hannibal, he was."

"That's not all," Dad added. "Here in England, there's been a rash of home invasions by people dressed in various historical costumes claiming the houses really belong to them and ordering the actual owners out onto the street."

"Lucinda has been at work, right?" said Adam. "It sounds like—"

"Adam!" Molly interrupted. "It's about time!" She had been waiting impatiently for him to come back in ever since she'd finally got out of bed. She'd awoken with a revelation, or as she liked to call it, a "light-bulb moment." Now that Adam was here, she could tell everyone about it at the same time.

"Come on," Reggie said to Adam, "you need to eat." The table was covered with Reggie's sumptuous breakfast.

"And I have something very, very important to tell everyone," Molly added. "Hurry!"

"Where's Granddad?" Adam asked, heading for the sink to wash the dirt off his hands.

"Granddad and Shorty and Brad have gone wherever they go to keep Lucinda away from us," said Dad. "They're planning to be very secretive and look like they're nervous about something, and Granddad is pretending to have something hidden inside his shirt pocket. We're hoping that she'll be curious about what they're up to and follow them, so that we can talk without her eavesdropping. Molly says she has something very important to tell us."

"Not as important as what I have to tell you!" Adam exclaimed.

"Yes, Adam," Molly said, "it is. It's very important."

"But I need to show you something while Lucinda isn't here," Adam continued, not waiting for Molly to stop him. "I found the p . . . the icebox!"

"The icebox?" said Mom

"What icebox?" said Dad.

"This one!" Adam said dramatically as he pulled the pendant out of his pocket.

It certainly had the desired effect. Everyone in the room gasped.

"That is some icebox, Adam," Reggie said. "Well done!"

"Adam! How on Earth?" said his mom.

"No way!" exclaimed Molly.

Adam's dad reached for the pendant and took it from him. He held it up to the light, where it sparkled brightly. Reggie rushed over, took off his ring and held it up beside the pendant. The two gems sparkled even more brightly when next to each other. And they were perfectly matched. They were the same shape—sort of like a leaf—and the same size, different only in the intense green of one and the intense blue of the other. There was no doubt. It was the Morning Eye.

"Adam," said his dad, "how did you get it?"

"Never mind that," Adam said nervously, looking this way and that around the room, "I'll tell you later. First, we need to find a way to hide it from Lucinda."

Before anyone could object Reggie had taken the pendant, lowered it over his head and tucked it under his crocodile-and-hula-dancer shirt.

"She couldn't get the ring from me," he said. "What could be safer?"

"I don't know, Reggie," Mom said. "I'm not sure that's a good idea. After all, if Lucinda captures you she'll have both gems in one place."

"And," added Molly, "if she can figure out how to break the spell, or whatever it is that stopped her from getting the ring before—well, then she'll have both of them."

"Molly's right," said Mom. "We should separate them."

"All right," Reggie agreed reluctantly, as he slowly took it off.

"I can keep it," said Molly, reaching out for it.

"No, Molly," said Mom, "not if I have anything to do with it. Give it here, Reggie." She put the pendant around her neck and tucked it under her sweater.

"No!" said Molly. "It's too dangerous!"

"And so you think you should have it instead of me?" Mom asked. "What kind of mother do you think I am, young lady?" She had that look on her face that meant she had made up her mind and that was that, there was nothing anyone else could possibly do about it.

Molly sighed and gave in.

"I don't know, Lily," said Dad uneasily. "I mean, wouldn't it be less dangerous if somebody wasn't actually wearing it?"

"We could bury it again," said Adam. "Put it back where it was."

"And just let Lucinda come and get it whenever she feels like it?" said Mom. "We need to know if and when she's trying."

"That does make sense," said Dad grudgingly.

"There's only one thing to do now," said Mom. "It stays right here." She patted her sweater.

"But Adam," said Dad. "How did you get hold of it? The p . . . the icebox, I mean."

"It was that little ghost, John," Adam explained. "It seems he took it from his mom's room as part of a game of pirates he was playing with a friend. He buried it—and then he died before he could return it!"

"So that's why nobody could ever find it," said Dad.

"Yeah," said Adam. "And it was out there in the backyard under a tree the whole time!"

Molly looked at Adam admiringly. She could have sworn she actually was proud of him.

"And," Adam concluded, "since he took the necklace from his mom and the person who owned the necklace was Maurice's wife, he must be Maurice's son!" He paused for a moment. "But, Molly," he said, "you said you had something important to tell us, too. What is it?"

Oh, right. In the excitement of Adam's discovery, she'd forgotten all about her own idea. "We need to find the elephant now more than ever!"

"Well, duh," said Adam.

Molly didn't feel quite so proud of him after that. She glared in his direction and said, "If you'd let me explain? As long as Reggie and Mom have the jewels—"

"The iceboxes," Reggie interrupted.

"The iceboxes," Molly repeated. "As long as they have them, they are personally in danger and of course so is the rest of the world, right?"

144

"Right." said Adam. "So?"

"So, I was thinking about the elephant—dreaming about it really, because I wasn't quite awake yet, despite all the racket made by certain people." She gave Adam an icy stare. "And," she continued, "I was wondering where Lucinda would have it and, well, it suddenly it occurred to me that she would have to hide it!"

"I don't see what you mean," said Adam.

"It's like this. She can't carry it around with her because she wants to keep going back and forth between this world and the ghostly one, right? At least that's what she's been doing, as we well know. And the thing is, she can't carry real objects into the ghostly world!"

"Good point, Molly," said Mom.

"That's what I thought," said Molly, throwing Adam an I-told-you-so look. "And if she couldn't keep it with her, she'd have to actually hide it somewhere in this world—somewhere she could easily get it." She paused again. "Get it? It must be around here somewhere! Here in Oxford!"

"That is logical," said Dad. "Well thought out, Molly."

"But what I want to know," said Adam, "is why she wouldn't just have destroyed it as soon as she got her hands on it."

"It's true," said Mom. "For all we know, it might not even exist anymore. In which case . . ."

"In which case," said Molly, "the world is already doomed. She can't have! She just can't have!"

"I think you're right about that, actually," said Adam. "I'm just not sure why. It's that poem. Something about that poem. 'And the living undone.'"

"Anyway," interrupted Molly, "until we know for sure, we have to keep acting as if the elephant does still exist, right?

"And," said Dad, "now that Adam has found the pendant—"

"The icebox," said Reggie.

"The icebox—we just have to keep looking for the elephant and trying to reunite it with the eyes," said Molly.

"But where do we start?" Adam asked. "Oxford is a big place."

"Maybe, we could find something in the library that would give us some hints," said Dad. "Maybe Lucinda's death notice or something about the theft— anything that might give us a clue."

This didn't surprise Molly at all; there was nowhere Dad would rather be than a library. And at least it gave them somewhere to start.

That's when Granddad appeared.

CHAPTER FOURTEEN
A Hunt for a Hint

"**S**horty and Bart have Lucinda trapped in a small time-space pocket," Granddad whispered, "but it won't last long. I just thought I'd find out what's going on here."

"What's a time-space pocket?" Adam asked.

"A sort of prison. It's very hard to explain," said Granddad. "Let's just say she hasn't got any idea where she is right now, and she isn't aware that time is passing at all."

"Neat," said Adam.

"It's actually rather untidy," said Granddad. "The hours get all tangled up and you're not sure if you're coming or going when, in fact, you're actually doing both at the same time. It's most unsettling. But what's happening?"

"We've found the icebox!" said Adam.

"Icebox?" said Granddad. "Were you looking for an icebox? Why?"

Molly's mom drew out the pendant and showed it to Granddad. "The icebox," she said. "This."

"Is that . . . ?" he asked, his eyes bugging out of his head.

She tucked it back in.

"It most certainly is," she said. "You can thank Adam."

Granddad turned to Adam. "How did you find it?"

Adam quickly told him about John and his pirate treasure game.

"Amazing!" said Granddad. "And it's a good thing we had Lucinda in that time prison, or she would have found out about it for sure. That woman has a nose for us Barnetts, no question about it. How on Earth do we keep the—the iceboxes? Yes, the iceboxes—away from Lucinda?"

For a moment no one spoke, but everyone was thinking feverishly.

"We need to throw her off the track," Molly finally said. "Act as if nothing has changed."

"What if we pretend we're still looking," said Adam, "so that when she comes nosing around she'll think it's still lost?"

"Yes," said Molly, "good idea. She'll keep looking for it, then, and not realize we already have it."

"I know," said Adam. "Mom, you and Reggie could

148

come up with a theory of where you think it is and go hunting for it."

"We could," Mom agreed, "but I really do think that Reggie and I should split up, so that if she does figure it out she'll still need to find each of us separately."

"And yet," said Reggie, "there is strength in numbers."

Molly knew that Reggie was dedicated to looking after Mom and didn't like the thought of her being on her own and at the mercy of Lucinda. She had to admit he had a point.

"I agree with Reggie," Molly said.

"So do I," Dad said firmly.

"Me, too," added Granddad just as firmly.

Adam felt the same way, and he said so. He knew quite well that Mom was no weakling, but Lucinda wasn't either and two against one were better odds.

Mom obviously knew what they were all thinking, and looked as if she was about to explode. But nobody flinched; they all just stared back at her. Finally, she sighed and nodded.

"It's as if feminism never happened," she said bitterly. "But okay, if you all insist. Why don't Reggie and I pretend to be looking around here," she said. "In the cottage, around the village, and so forth. And while we're doing it—together, of course—well, Tim, you can take the kids in the car and go searching for more information in the library."

"The library?" asked Granddad. "Why the library?"

Dad quickly explained his idea.

"I see," said Granddad. "Excellent. I'll check things out over on the other side and then after that I'll meet you at the library, Timmie." He disappeared.

"But before we get started," Reggie said, "I insist that everyone finish their breakfast. This is going to be a busy day."

It sounded like a good idea to Adam. He sat down and began to help himself to a plateful of eggs, bacon, sausage, beans, and toast. But for once he couldn't concentrate on his food. He sat at the table as everyone around him ate, a thoughtful look on his face.

Suddenly, his eyes lit up and he leaped to his feet.

"Eureka!" he said gleefully. "I have it!"

"Have what?" Molly asked. He looked as if what he had was a bad case of sugar high—and as far as she knew, he'd had hardly any sugar.

"It's the poem!" he said. "It's why I know Lucinda hasn't destroyed the elephant yet!"

"What are you talking about, Adam?" His dad said as he came back into the kitchen from a trip to the bathroom.

"I've been thinking and thinking about it," Adam said.

"As we know," said Molly. He'd been on about that stupid poem and the elephant ever since they'd arrived in England yesterday.

"Well, Molly," he said, "you should be glad I was—because I've figured it out. It's the lines in the poem that go,

'But apart, and the heart
Of the world will unfurl
And chaos shall come
And the loud shall be dumb,
And the living undone.'

"'And the living undone,'" Adam repeated with emphasis. "What do you think that means?"

"I don't know!" said Molly in a fit of exasperation. "You're the poem expert, Adam. What do you think it means?"

"I think, Molly, that it means exactly what it says—that while the eyes remain separated, the dead are more and more likely to come back to life—and, and this is the important part, the living are more likely to stop living—to be 'undone.' Get it?"

"I . . . I think so," said Molly. "But—but our great-great-granddad Maurice had the eyes removed from the elephant a hundred years ago or so, and people kept on living after that, right? And, and we're still alive, right?"

"So far," said Adam. "But it also took a hundred years for . . . for someone . . . to figure out what the curse meant and let a ghost like Lucinda know about it."

"Or," Mom interjected, "it just took a hundred years for the curse to really start working." They all knew how badly Adam felt about figuring out what that poem meant and then explaining it to Molly while Lucinda was eavesdropping.

"Mom's right, Adam," said Molly. "I mean, it took a long time to get started, but it does seem to be getting faster—all this stuff happening, I mean. First, Lucinda had to occupy other people's minds, but then we could see her—and finally she could get her own real body back. And now there are all these people on the news meeting ghosts everywhere. It's like a snowball rolling down a hill."

"I suppose," said Adam. "Anyway, the dead didn't start coming back to their bodies till now—and I think that means we can expect living people to start leaving their bodies now as well."

"Adam," said Dad, "That's horrible; logical, but horrible."

"And accurate," said Granddad as he blinked into view by the kitchen door. "There seems to be a new influx of lost souls suddenly appearing on the astral plane. I've met five or six of them myself already, including a new couple just now. They all seem to think they're still alive and in their bodies, and can't figure out why suddenly they aren't able to hit the keys of their computers or operate their cars. And others around the astral plane have been reporting similar incidents everywhere."

"Come to think of it," said Dad, "there was a report on the news this morning about an increasing percentage of sudden heart failure here in the U.K. and also in the U.S. and India. Apparently, the medical authorities can't account for it and are searching for a previously unknown virus."

"That is unbelievable," said Molly, horrified. "It's like a murder curse or something. And," she added, "it has nothing to do with Lucinda, in a way. I mean, in fact, if Granddad hadn't come back and we hadn't discovered Lucinda, people would be dying now and we would have no idea why. So in a way it's good at least that we know what's going on."

Adam looked doubtful, but Molly didn't want him to feel responsible for destroying the world or for anyone dying. And anyway, she meant what she had just said. It really wasn't his fault at all.

"I'm afraid it's the original fellow who created the curse who's to blame," said her dad. "And I don't suppose we'll ever find out who that was. I mean, even Maurice, who separated the eyes and put the curse in motion, can't really be blamed, can he? I mean, who would believe such nonsense?"

"That's someone else Granddad should be looking for on the astral plane," said Molly. "the person who created the curse and started all this."

"Yes, indeed," said Reggie, his eyes blazing fury.

"But," said Adam, "if people are suddenly dying, at least it means that Lucinda hasn't destroyed the elephant yet. Or, at least, that's what I think."

"How do you work that out, Adam?" asked Mom. "I don't follow."

"Me neither," said Reggie.

"Lucinda's no dummy, right? I mean, she figured out what to do when she learned about the curse with no trouble at all. And she's been clever enough to get the right kind of people on her side—people like that knight, Sir Eustace."

"That's true," said Molly. Adam seemed to be thinking in a surprisingly logical way. Maybe there was hope for him yet.

"So I'm thinking," Adam continued, "that she's also figured out the part about the living being undone. Or if she hasn't," he added in a much louder voice as he glared up toward the ceiling, "with any luck she'll overhear me talking about it right now!"

It would certainly be good for Adam if she did, thought Molly. It'd sort of make up for him spilling the beans to her back in Palm Springs.

"She can't destroy the elephant," Adam continued loudly, "because then she won't have it in case the curse starts working at full speed. If that happens, everyone on the planet will be 'undone' and will die—including the spirits who were dead already, like herself because the whole world will just come to a complete and total end—like an empty void. If that starts to happen, Lucinda can always try sticking the eyes back—as long as she still has them *and* the elephant. She needs to keep them as a backup, just in case!" He was shouting now. "She really, really does!"

So it wasn't just bad times they were trying to save the world from—it was even worse. It was annihilation.

It did make sense, Molly thought, excellent sense. Almost irrefutable. So the elephant did still exist—must, surely, still exist, if Lucinda had any sense left at all—and they did still have a chance to save the world, not just from disaster, but from extinction. But did Lucinda have any sense left? Maybe she didn't care about the world as long as she had her revenge.

Maybe, thought Molly, maybe the time had come for them to get the authorities involved—the police or the army or the Mounties, or the CIA, or the prime minister of Britain or the president of the United States. Surely they needed all the help they could get.

But no. It all sounded way too weird. Nobody was going to believe them until it was too late.

So, it was up to them: the Barnetts and the Crankshafts. They just had to find the elephant—and find it quickly, before too many living people died and too many dead people started living again. And dying again. They had to get the two eyes back where they belonged!

As Molly dug into the plate of bacon and eggs and toast Reggie had put in front of her, her mind was racing. Where could the elephant be? Where might Lucinda think of hiding it?

A new thought struck her. She was so stupid! She swallowed her mouthful of eggs, took a swig of orange juice and said, "It has to be close to where she stole it from!"

"Yes, Mol, we know," said Dad, "You told us about that earlier—about how she could only carry it when she was in her body, because she wouldn't be able to pick it up when she was on the astral plane."

"But I didn't get the whole thing then. What it really meant."

Everyone looked at her.

"When she stole it from that lady she had to find somewhere close to hide it, right? Like for instance, she couldn't have brought it all the way out here to Toot Baldon; it'd be too far to go."

"Not unless she wanted to commandeer a car," said Reggie ruefully. "And bully the driver into taking her there."

"But she wouldn't want to attract too much attention," said Molly. "Not yet, anyway. So she had to hide it somewhere close by, somewhere she could walk to!"

"Brilliant, Molly," said Mom. "It could just be buried in the garden behind the house she stole it from."

"Or somewhere down the street from it, maybe,"

added Molly.

"Or," said Reggie, "that college where she hid me. Yes, of course! According to what you told me yesterday, it's only a few blocks away from there, right?"

"Yes," said Adam, "but why—?"

"Hold on a minute," said Reggie, "and I'll explain. See, I know it sounds a little strange—but, well, I was wondering why she picked that place. To hide me in, I mean. It's inside the college, past the porter, down the stairs, hidden in the dark—how would a maid like her, who'd probably never even gone to school, let alone college, even know about a little place like that? It isn't likely she'd ever have been in New College when she was alive, back when the colleges were all-male places. And yet she seemed to know it really well. In fact, she knew exactly where to put me."

"I suppose it's a possibility," said Dad. "We can certainly put it on our list. And hey, New College is just a short distance away from the Bodleian Library. How about we head in that direction, and then we can split up? The rest of you can try to get in and take a look down there in the dungeon while I see what I can find in the Bodleian. I know there are old newspaper archives for sure, and there might be some documents about local residents, too. Maybe I can dig up something about Lucinda that'll help us."

Molly wasn't surprised by her dad's suggestion, and not just because he loved libraries and practically lived in them when he was researching his documentaries. He especially loved the Bodleian, which she'd often heard him talk about with a longing look in his eyes. And his plan suited her just fine. Reggie was right—there was something about that dungeon, something that needed further investigation.

Adam seemed all right with it, too, although Molly found it hard to tell, as he was totally immersed in his full English. Now that he'd finally got his idea about the poem out of his head and off his chest, he was back to his old self again.

"You know," Reggie said slowly, "I never got to see the place she put me in. It was pitch dark down there, but it seemed to be pretty large. Maybe you should check in there."

"That knight, Sir Eustace, might still be in the corridor," Adam pointed out. "If she hasn't told him about getting his body back, I mean. He did have a tie to that dungeon, didn't he? Something about Mary Queen of Scots, wasn't it? He wasn't there just to scare us off from finding Reggie."

"Well then," said Molly, "we'll just have to figure out a way to distract him."

"Okay, kidlets," said Dad as he grabbed one more sausage from the almost-empty plate on the table, "let's get going."

CHAPTER FIFTEEN
Regal Haunts

Once in the car and finished with the last piece of toast he'd brought along, Adam had time to reflect on the whole plan, especially the part of it where Dad had said "Let's split up." Hadn't he seen any real movies? Not documentaries like he made himself, but ones where stuff happened? Whenever people split up in the movies, disaster struck. And usually someone ended up extremely dead. He didn't want that to be any of them; he particularly didn't want it to be him.

And what if Lucinda had shown Sir Eustace how to materialize into his own body by now, and that sharp sword had become all too real? Sharp steel versus human flesh? The sword would win, every time. This whole plan seemed a little, well, under-thought, like undercooked meat. Which he hated, all red and gory, like head cheese before it got turned into solidified gore jelly. Like victims of sharp swords. He shuddered just thinking about it.

But, he thought with a sigh, there was no way to get out of it now. Granddad had headed back off to the astral plane to try to keep tabs on Lucinda, saying he'd do his best to keep her occupied and try to warn them if she was likely to pop up anywhere. Mom and Reggie had decided to stay in the cottage and pretend to look for the pendant—making sure they had a phone with them so they could keep in touch. The plan might just keep Lucinda out of their hair.

Or, thought Adam, at least keep the jewels away from her while she was in their hair.

And now Dad was about to head off to the library, and he and Molly would be totally on their own.

But he wasn't going to change anyone's mind just because he was scared. That really wasn't a good enough reason—even he realized that.

And anyway, it was going to be a lot scarier when all the ghosts did materialize. From what they'd seen so far, the only dead people who were still hanging around and acting ghostly were unhappy or angry or tied to the Earthly plane for some reason. So when they got their bodies back, they'd all be disturbed and hysterical, like John, or very bad, like Lucinda. So what kind of army could fight the bad guys? Sure, there were bound to be a few good guys still alive to fight on their side, but nevertheless, they were bound to be heavily outnumbered.

And, it seemed, if Granddad and Adam himself were right about what the poem meant, chaos had come and the loud had turned dumb and the living were undone. Some of the good guys were already dying.

No, things definitely were not looking good.

"Hey, you!" Dad suddenly shouted. "Move your ##@@, you stupid #$%^%^#$#! Now!"

Adam looked up to see a huge man standing in the middle of the road, dressed like an ancient monarch or something, hands planted firmly on his hips. He stared right back through the windshield at Adam, a sneer on his face as the car rushed ahead.

Dad gave the wheel a quick turn, just in time to avoid actually hitting the man. As the car zoomed past him, Adam could have sworn that it actually grazed the man's fat belly. Still swearing a blue streak, Dad screeched the car over to the side and leaped out, followed by Adam and Molly.

Immediately, the fellow in the middle of the road stalked over to them and bellowed, "Bow down, subjects!"

Adam stared at him. He was something to stare at, that was for sure. He had a red beard and a very large stomach, which stuck out in front of him, and he was dressed up like one of the old British lords or kings—a flowery lacy hat, a kind of jewel-covered mini-dress under a fur-lined coat with puffy sleeves, and some dark pantyhose. He was covered in huge necklaces and the rings on his hands gleamed and sparkled. He was dressed up just like one of those skinny actresses on a red carpet, thought Adam, all sparkly and frilly—but somehow, for all the jewels and the frilly dress, he didn't look at all girlish.

"Bow down, We said," he repeated, waving the short sword he held in his hand. "Bow down, now!" The voice had such authority that Adam almost did.

"What is this place?" the large man asked, glaring imperiously at them. "We do not like it here. It looks all . . . all very strange. And that machine of yours is very noisy and very ugly."

"And very dangerous," Dad said angrily. "You just nearly got yourself killed there, buddy."

"We are not buddy, varlet!" the man said. "And did We not say 'bow'? BOW!"

This time, Adam found himself falling to his knees. He looked around to see what Molly and his dad were doing. Molly was glaring at the fellow defiantly; Dad, still swearing under his breath, was trying to get in front of both of them, probably to protect them from the man's sword.

"Don't listen to him," said a young woman who'd just appeared beside the large man. "He's all talk. Talk! talk! talk! 'We don't like this' and 'We demand that' and 'We are not amused.' Silly old blowhard!" She gave the large man a dismissive look and crossed her arms over her chest.

Molly could see that this new arrival was also dressed in old-fashioned clothes—not like Lucinda's, Molly thought, but older, like in the days of yore, and encrusted with all sorts of jewels and embroidery. She also wore lots of rings and necklaces, and she was as slim as the man was big, with delicate features and dark shining hair pulled up by a glittering diamond thingy on her head. Molly was sure she must be some sort of queen.

"You?" said the large man, turning to her with angry fire in his eyes. "What are you doing here? Why are you here?"

"The usual reason, good sire," she said with a harsh laugh. "I know how much you hate me being around. So naturally, I do my best to be with you always—as you well know."

"Indeed," he said angrily. "Indeed We do."

"So," she continued with an impish smile, "when I noticed you coming here, I had no choice but to follow."

"Follow you may," he bellowed, "but not for long!" With a sudden sweep of his sword, he slashed at her neck.

As the young woman's head separated from her body, she blinked out of view. But only for a moment—just long enough for Molly to stare in horror at the place where she'd been standing. Then, almost immediately, she was back again.

"Hah!" she said. "You have no power over me anymore, you tickle-brained fat-belly! You beef-witted jolt head! See?"

With that, she put her hands on her head and removed it, disappeared once more, and returned once more.

"Still here!" she said triumphantly. "How does that feel, you bloated malodorous pigeon egg?"

Molly remembered Granddad doing that a few times—dying and disappearing, then turning back into a visible ghost again right before their eyes. Was this woman just a ghost, then, like Granddad? Molly reached out toward her and felt for her dress.

Nothing—her hand went right through. So the woman didn't have a real body, not right now at least. Nor, with any luck, did the large man she was now laughing at. He was busy screaming insults at her.

"Anne," he shouted, "you are a foul maggot pie!"

"And what kind of a worm deprives his own sweet daughter of a mother?"

The big fellow looked a bit pale—if a ghost could look pale.

"You deserved it!" he screamed at her. "Venomed flap-mouthed bladder!"

"That's what you are," she said calmly. "But what about me?" She laughed again. "Your trouble, you know," she added, "is that you just couldn't stand having a woman around who spoke back to you, who was well-read, who had thoughts of her own."

"You couldn't give me a male heir," he shot back.

The woman's voice grew quiet as she walked up to him and faced him nose to nose. "And who ended up being the greatest queen ever? Was it your precious son? Or was it our daughter—our poor orphaned daughter Elizabeth?"

Elizabeth? And the head coming off and . . . and . . . Molly knew who it was!

"Henry the Eighth?" she exclaimed.

"And Anne Boleyn?" Dad added in amazement.

"At your service," she said, with an imperious nod.

"Not at *their* service," said Henry, "you mangled fool-born jolthead! At mine! You may be dead, but We are still your monarch. Bow down! Now!"

"Never," she said. And she reached up to the top of her head again, pulled it off, and waved it right in his face, her tongue sticking out at him and nearly licking his nose.

"Onion-eyed mumble-news!" he said, and stuck his own tongue out, right back at her. For a moment the two of them stared at each other, in a battle to see who would blink first.

Anne won. Henry blinked and pulled in his tongue. "We will remain here no longer," he declared. "Our task is accomplished. These fools"—he made a sweeping gesture toward Adam and Molly and their dad—"have been delayed. We will return now to our leader."

Leader? Who could that be, Molly wondered. Not anybody the king had much respect for, clearly—he had said "leader" with absolute scorn.

"You do that," said Anne. "But I've my eye on you."

"Ooh, We are so scared," said Henry as he blinked out.

"He really is scared, you know," Anne said. "Of me, a mere woman. Cowardly old blubberguts!" Laughing, she blinked out as well.

Dad shook his head. "Unreal," he said. "As if we don't have enough to deal with, now Lucinda is bringing back truly dangerous, powerful people."

"And," said Adam, "they want to slow us down, for some reason. That can't be good."

"And that 'leader' he was talking about," added Molly. "Do you think it's Lucinda?"

"It must be," said Adam. "Who else would try to push that blowhard around?"

"Come on," said Dad, "let's get back to what we were about to do—without delay. The sooner we find of way of ending all this, the better."

They piled back in the car. And since Molly was in charge of the directions her dad had downloaded from the computer, she concentrated on getting them through town efficiently. Meanwhile, Adam sat and wondered who else Lucinda had recruited and what else could be in store for them when they reached New College. Why did she want to delay them? Did she have something up her sleeve?

"Okay, Dad," Molly said, "when you get to the roundabout, take the second right."

"I hate roundabouts," said Dad. "Round and round and round they go, and where they stop nobody knows. I think that they ought to be banned from the face of the globe." He added a few more of his signature curses.

Molly managed to keep reading out the directions and steering her dad past a surprising number of bad choices. It seemed like an eternity before they finally came to the barrier at the start of Holywell Street.

"Now what?" said Dad. "Where do I park?"

"Up there, I guess," said Molly, pointing up a street without a barrier. But they had to drive quite a while before they actually found a legal space.

As they got out of the car and began to walk back toward New College her dad said, "Here we are trying to save the world and we might well be stopped by too many roundabouts and too much red tape about where you can and cannot park!"

Molly thought it would be too bad if that turned out to be true. Unless Lucinda had got somebody to paint all these double lines just to delay them more? The paint did look quite fresh.

"You're likely to take less time searching that dungeon than I'm going to spend in the library," Dad continued. "How about you come over and meet me there? I'll tell the receptionist to expect you. Or who knows?

I might find something really quickly, in which case I'll come and join you."

And with that he strode off down the street, looking distinctly happier at the thought of soon being in a library.

"How are we going to get in?" Adam asked as they headed around the corner to the gate they'd used yesterday. All he could see of the college from where they were walking was a lot of very high stone walls. "That is, if that ghost isn't hanging around waiting for us with his sword already drawn." Perhaps that was why Lucinda had sent Henry after them? To give her time to bring back Sir Eustace's body?

Molly gave her brother the look she always gave him when she thought he was being silly. "Really, Adam," she said. "We'll just find that porter guy, and . . . and . . . "

"Tell him your friend lost something in that room when he was shut in there," Dad shouted from halfway down the road—he must have thought about the problem of them getting in just when Adam did. Then he turned and headed off toward the library.

Now Adam was really depressed. There seemed to be no way to stop this plan—this very dangerous plan. And sure enough, all too quickly they were at the gate they had been at before, and Molly had no trouble in finding a porter in the office beside the gate, although not the porter they'd met yesterday.

"That was old Harold," said the porter when Molly inquired. "He's off to a cricket match today."

Still, this porter—a tall, thin man with thick white hair and thicker white eyebrows and a big white Band-Aid on his forehead whose name turned out to be George—had heard all about what had happened the day before from Harold, and he treated Molly and Adam as if they were old friends.

"That was a real hubble-bubble yesterday!" he said. "Now wasn't it just?"

Molly nodded, and went on to tell him her story about Reggie being the subject of an undergraduate prank, and how he'd lost one of his cufflinks.

George bought the whole thing without even winking.

"I know all about those pranks," he said with a grin. "And well I might, after twenty-five years here at the gate. Why, one time I nearly got electrocuted trying to open the door to the Muniment Tower—some students had electrified the doorknob, you see—an old, old prank but still unfortunately popular. Then there was the time when some of the fourth years brought an elephant into the quadrangle—an actual elephant! Can you imagine?"

Adam shivered. Was it just a coincidence that the porter was talking about an elephant? Or . . . something else.

"Stole it from a travelling circus in Reading, they

did," the porter continued, "and made it walk all the way here, poor old thing, and left it to graze atop The Mound. It took us weeks to get the lawns back in shape."

After George took a very long time to find his keys and then called someone else to come look after the gate, he led them into the cloisters, and then into the darkness of the stairway heading down to the dungeon.

On the stairs, Adam sighed, and then took a deep breath. He wished he had armour on. He kept thinking about the knight.

As they followed the porter down the wide stone steps and then to the thick door, all was quiet except for the sound of their feet on the stones and Molly's endless chatter.

"Yes, and Reggie had on this ring and he says he dropped it and we really want to find it for him, and this is just so nice of you, we're so impressed by how nice everyone in Oxford is, and . . ."

George turned the key to the door and pushed it open. He flicked on the lights.

Adam's jaw dropped. What was all this?

CHAPTER SIXTEEN
Elephant Hunt

George grinned at Adam, pleased he was so surprised. "Didn't see this before?" he said. "You must have been in such a hurry to leave that you didn't notice what was here."

"We certainly didn't," said Molly. She too was stunned.

The room they could now see so clearly was about fifteen feet square, with a stone floor and a barrel ceiling. The one small window was covered by a black velvet curtain. The room was filled with glass cabinets containing objects that caught the light and twinkled. Framed papers and cloths covered the walls. Adam wasn't sure what any of it was.

"With the lights out," George said, "it's very lucky your friend didn't crash into any of it and destroy something. He is rather—big—isn't he?" He paused.

"Or so I heard."

Adam had to allow that Reggie certainly was big, and that it was a bit of a miracle that nothing had been broken. "But," he added, "why are all these things hidden down here?"

"Hardly hidden," replied George. "This is the college museum, this is. It may not be the Ashmolean, but it's ours, and we're right proud of it." He gazed around the room with pride.

"Wow," said Molly, "it might not be hidden but, well, on the other hand, it isn't exactly on display, is it?"

George smiled. He'd obviously taken a liking to her. "It's always open to guests of the college," he said. "Let me give you the tour."

Molly smiled back at him. Adam crossed his fingers behind his back, and hoped the tour wouldn't take too long—or attract the attention of Sir Eustace.

George waved his arms around the room. "These, my young friends, are the college treasures," he boasted.

"Treasures?" Adam asked. That reminded him of little John's game of pirates. But these things didn't look much like the stuff a pirate would want; it seemed to be just old cream jugs and plates and things.

"Yes," said George, "treasures. Most of them are things that people have given to the college over the centuries—former students and dignitaries and such.

Why, if you think about it, these things tell the entire history of New College!"

If they do, thought Adam, it must have been a boring history, involving a lot of tea drinking and silver polish. Which, incidentally, a lot of these things could have used. They were downright filthy.

"And yet," George went on, "surprisingly few people seem to understand how interesting these precious items are."

Yeah, thought Adam, about as surprising as mosquitoes back home in August and about as precious, too.

"Oh, dear," said Molly, very politely.

"Indeed," said George. "After each dinner here, you know, it's the custom for the warden to ask his guests if any of them would like to see the treasures. Mostly people say no, which I'm afraid is a great relief to him." His voice lowered into a whisper. "I hate to say this, you know, but he finds it a bother coming down here. It's not like the old days. Not at all."

"Oh, dear," said Molly again.

"Hardly anybody ever visits the treasures nowadays. Still," he added a little more cheerfully, "the occasional guest does request to see them. The silver is especially fine. This, for instance," he pointed to something in the case they were standing by that looked like a metal book, "is a silver and parcel-gilt pax from the sixteenth century. And this beside it is the Monkey Salt."

"Monkey Salt?" asked Adam. It looked sort of like a giant gold chess piece with an ape face.

"Yes," George replied. "It's actually meant to hold salt, even though it's in the shape of a monkey. They knew how to make things back in them days."

Molly nodded. Adam tried not to snort. The Monkey Salt was really, really ugly. And huge. The thing was about a foot high. People back then must have liked to use a lot of salt.

"And look here," George said, the excitement in his voice rising as he moved to another case. "Here are our unicorn horns!"

Unicorn horns! Now that was something to be excited about! Adam looked into the case. He saw two long hunks of old brown stuff. They did sort of look like horns, if you closed your eyes and squinted.

"Before the college got hold of them," said George, "these two were presented by Sir Walter Raleigh to Queen Elizabeth the First. If you make a wish on them, it's sure to come true."

Adam wondered if there could be any truth to that. Most people probably assumed it was just a legend. But what if the horns really could grant a wish? If they could, he knew exactly what to wish for. It was quite small, and ivory. He wished he could find that cursed elephant.

"Naturally," continued George, "they're really just the tusks of some animal, perhaps walrus—or even elephant tusks."

Elephant tusks! Elephants again!

But not the right elephant.

"It is a wonderful story," George added. "I do indeed think it is."

"Indeed," said Molly with a fixed smile.

"And over here," George said from in front of yet another case, "here's a really important piece, if I do say so myself."

Why wouldn't he say so himself? Adam wondered.

"The brave fellow who wore this helmet fought for Cromwell against the evil king, he did. Gave his life for the glorious cause, he did. Look, it has a hole right through the front. That must have hurt. Hurt very badly."

Adam really didn't want to think about that too much. It reminded him of Sir Eustace.

"And yet," George continued, "it was all for nought. The king won anyway, curse him! So much sacrifice, and for so little return. It's enough to make a person angry, it is! Very, very angry."

George did indeed seem to be getting very excited. His face was turning red, and he was actually shaking.

"Are you okay?" Molly asked.

"Don't worry, Miss," said George, clearly trying to control his shakes. "It just, well, I'm an old soldier myself, see. Seen too much of the horrors of war in person, I have. Know too much about how they treat you after you're no more use to them. After you've been

maimed. After you've been ruined for much of anything." He was shaking even more now, and was very
red. "It makes me so angry, it makes me want to——"

"Molly! Adam!"

Dad burst into the room. "I've found it!" He looked
at the porter. "Oh, hello." He put out his hand to shake
the porter's and said, "I'm their dad, Tim Barnett."

"How do you do?" said George, shaking Tim's hand.
He was still trying to calm himself down. "I . . . I was
just showing your children the treasure room, and I
guess we must have got carried away and forgot the
time. The things down here are really so interesting."
He turned to Molly with a smile. "Aren't they?"

"Oh, yes," said Molly, "Fascinating." She hoped he
believed her——it was obvious that *he* certainly found
the treasures fascinating in a creepy sort of way. She
didn't want to set him off onto another tirade. It
seemed blood was actually beginning to seep from the
bandage on his forehead.

"I do apologize for keeping them," said George,
now completely calm and exuding charm. "I don't suppose you'd like to take a look yourself, Sir?"

"Actually," said Dad with a glance around the room,
"I've been down here before——back when I was an
undergraduate. Made the warden bring me here when
he offered to——as a joke! The poor old chap was hoping
to watch a Monty Python rerun and was quite furious
with me."

George gave their dad a look as if he weren't quite following.

"But," added Dad, "the treasures really are fascinating, and I certainly wouldn't mind taking another peek. I seem to recall a quite wonderful coconut cup."

He would, thought Molly. He was such a sucker for history.

"And," George pointed out eagerly, "this here helmet—"

"But right now," Dad added, "I—"

"Oh, yes," George interrupted. "I nearly forgot. The children were supposed to be looking for something, weren't they?"

"Yes," said Dad with some urgency, "but that's not why I—"

"Oh, yes," said Molly, "We were, and I didn't forget, Dad—despite how fascinating the things are and all. I've been looking in the cases and on the floor and everywhere, but haven't seen anything. Not yet."

"Me either," said Adam, who had actually been too busy being frightened of knights and making wishes on unicorns to have done any looking.

"Just listen to me for a minute!" Dad exclaimed impatiently. "She died here!"

"Huh?" said Molly.

Adam asked, "Who?"

"Lucinda!" said their dad. "That's what I rushed over here to tell you."

"Died here?" Molly repeated.

"In this very spot," said Dad. "I found out about it in the first place I looked—thank goodness for Internet archives, eh? They make it so easy to search for things. Anyway, I figured I'd just take a chance and see if her name ever appeared in the *Times*—not likely for a maid, but it's always a good first step, so I fed it in and what do you know? There she was! The story said she had been found here with her children—it obviously created quite a stir, to make it into the *Times* like that. But I suppose it would, even today, if a woman and two children were found dead inside a college."

"It would indeed," said George, who had been following the conversation with much interest. "The warden would not be the least bit happy about it. Imagine— people dying right here in the crypt, right under the chapel!"

Adam did imagine it, and found himself shivering. People were supposed to be dead before they were brought to the crypt.

"Shoddy portering, that is," George added. "Letting people sneak in and die, I mean. Not a good thing for the college, not at all. But it was certainly not in my time."

"Yes," Dad told him. "It was long before."

"Well, actually," said George—and then he paused. "Yes, Sir," he added. "Long before."

"Did the paper say what happened?" asked Molly.

"At first," said Dad, "they thought it was foul play. They grilled all the undergraduates about it, and the professors, too, and came up with nothing. There wasn't anything to find, it seems. Nobody at the college even knew who she was."

How sad, thought Molly.

"Finally," Dad went on, "they concluded that she'd just brought her children into the chapel during a service for warmth. They'd been thrown out of the small room they'd all been living in over a shop on Broad Street because she could no longer afford the rent, and they had nowhere else to go. It seems no one would hire her after word about the missing necklace got out."

And yet, Molly reminded herself, Lucinda hadn't stolen the necklace. It had been under the tree where John had buried it the whole time. Instead of digging it up, he'd gotten sick and died—and that ended up killing two other children, too. And Lucinda, who was perfectly innocent, just as she'd said. No wonder she was still so angry, all these years later.

"They hid upstairs in the chapel at first," said Dad. "Then she snuck down here in the darkness, after everyone else had left the building. And then, one by one, they died. They think Lucinda last, after her children."

For the first time since they had met Lucinda, Molly found herself feeling sorry for her and understanding her better. After all, she had watched her own children die.

In a way, it was Lucinda's own fault for stealing, and thus losing her job. True, she hadn't stolen the ring or the pendant, but she had stolen plenty of other things, and that's why Reggie's ancestor Fitzie hadn't felt the need to stick up for her when she was accused of stealing the emerald ring that Fitzie had actually taken himself for safekeeping.

She must have felt so guilty about her children.

Or maybe she didn't. Maybe she just had a grudge against the people she worked for, for anybody who was better off than she was. Or maybe, when she saw her children suffer like that, she couldn't stand to think it had been her fault in any way. Which was probably why she blamed Molly's family.

Not that it was right for Lucinda to have murdered all those generations of Barnetts—including Molly's very own granddad. Not to mention Lucinda's attempts to add Dad to her list—and eventually, even, Adam. But it did explain some things.

"So she is definitely connected to this place," said Adam, "just like Molly said. Good thinking, Mol."

"Thank you, Adam," she said. It was nice to be right.

"Which means there is a good chance that the elephant's here."

"But," said Dad, with another anxious look at all the glass cases, "where do we start?"

"Let's just start," said Molly. "I'll begin at this end; Dad, you take that end. And George and Adam can ·

take the middle cases."

Molly knew that if she used "that" voice—the one that she and her mom shared—no one would argue with her. But this time it didn't work.

"I don't think so, Molly," said Dad.

"Huh? Why not?"

"It won't be necessary. I'm looking at our elephant right now."

CHAPTER SEVENTEEN

A Bloody Haunt for a Hunt

Molly couldn't believe it. Was it really going to be this easy? She moved over to her dad to see what he was pointing at, as did Adam.

It was an object sitting in a shadow beside a shiny dagger. It was, indeed, an elephant, a very small one carved from ivory—and instead of eyes, there were indentations. No wonder Maurice had taken out the eyes, thought Molly; the jewels had been the only special thing about the figure, and with them gone, it really wasn't much to look at.

The three Barnetts were speechless. George wasn't.

"Odd," he said. "No one has the key to these cases but us porters—which means me today—and I haven't lent it to anyone. How could that possibly have gotten in there?"

Well, that's easy, thought Molly—especially if you knew Lucinda. All she had to do was sneak in when the porter was dozing on the job, take the key, open the glass and put the elephant in the case, and then return the key.

But the question on Molly's mind was, why? Lucinda must surely have realized that, sooner or later, they'd get the idea to hunt for the elephant here. So wasn't it all just too obvious?

Something about this was too easy. Molly was starting to get a funny feeling. The hair on her neck stood up and she had goosebumps, too. It wasn't logical— not at all.

Adam and her Dad, however, were ecstatic.

"That's it!" said Dad.

"It has to be!" said Adam.

"It is! It is! It is!" they both shouted, doing a strange little hopping dance together and waving their arms up above their heads.

"Can you get it out?" Dad said to George.

"Of course," George answered. "I've got the keys. But what is it?"

"It's an elephant that belongs to my family," Dad answered. "Or rather, it belonged to my family."

"Belonged?"

"Yes," said Dad. "You see, we had an estate sale after my mother died last year."

"My condolences," said George.

"Thank you. Anyway, the elephant got into the sale."

"By accident," said Adam.

"Yes," said Dad, "by accident. And someone bought it. A woman named Martha Garryty-Smythe-Lowing."

"Oh," said George, sounding suspicious. "I see. So, it isn't yours after all."

"But it is," said Dad, "because Ms. Garryty-Smythe-Lowing agreed to sell it back to us."

"Except she couldn't," said Adam, "because when she went to look for it, it wasn't there."

"Stolen," said Dad.

"Stolen?" George said. "I don't like the sound of that! Tsk tsk."

"No, of course you don't," said Dad. "Me either. We've been looking everywhere for it—that's actually why we came here today."

Now George was looking even more suspicious. "But you said—"

"It's true," Adam interrupted, desperate to change the subject. "You can ask the auctioneers."

"Messinger and Messinger," Dad added. "Right here in Oxford. They can confirm the elephant belonged to my mother. And, well, if you can just get it out of the case, and let us take a closer look, we'd be grateful."

"And while we're doing that," said Adam, "you can call the auction house and Martha Garryty-Smythe-Lowing. They'll tell you that what we're saying is true."

185

"And," Dad added, "I'm sure they'll confirm that it's all right for us to take possession of it. I'm sure they will. Does that seem reasonable?"

George paused for a moment and gave Adam's dad a piercing stare, his lips pursed. It was clear he wasn't at all convinced.

Well, Adam thought, you had to admit—it did sound a little far-fetched. But he crossed his fingers again, hoping that George would believe them. Because if he didn't—well, they were going to have to get hold of the elephant one way or another. And any other way wasn't likely to be good for George's health, or theirs, for that matter.

A brief picture of Dad smashing the glass case and brandishing one of the unicorn horns over George's white-haired head flashed through Adam's mind. George would probably start bleeding even more.

"Yes," said George finally, "it does seem reasonable."

And with that, he pulled a huge set of keys off of his belt, chose one, and unlocked the case. He pulled the elephant out and handed it to Dad.

Dad looked at his children and smiled a very, very big smile.

"We've won!" he said.

"Now if you will just write those numbers down for me," said George, "I'll nip up to the office and call these people on that talking machine up there. You can look around the collection while I do that."

Shouldn't George at least keep the elephant until he made the calls? And Molly wondered why had he just said that the phone was a "talking machine"?

Saving the world ought to be more complicated, surely?

George left, closing the door behind him. As soon as he did so, Molly heard a kind of grinding sound from behind the door. It sounded like . . . like . . .

Like a key turning in a lock. Exactly like a key turning in a lock.

"Of course," she said, smacking herself on the forehead. "I knew it was too easy. He just locked us in."

"Don't be silly, Molly," said her dad. "Why would he do that?"

"I'm not sure," she said.

Her dad walked over to the thick door and tried to turn the handle. It was locked all right.

"I'm afraid you're right. Darn."

It was obvious Dad wasn't terribly upset—he almost never said anything as mild as "darn."

"But that's okay," he continued. "We'll just wait until he has it all straightened out and then we'll be free to leave—and by tonight we'll have the two gems back in the elephant and the world will be saved!"

"Yes!" said Adam. He was about to start his victory dance again when Molly shushed him.

"I hear something else," she said. "Don't you?"

Molly had excellent hearing. Adam stopped and listened carefully. Nothing. No, wait a minute—there was something. A mouse scurrying around in the darkness behind the cases, perhaps, or . . .

"It's coming from there," Molly said, pointing to the back of the room.

They hurried over. Sure enough, there was a noise coming from behind a door—a kind of muffled sound, a person trying to shout maybe. A person trying to call for help.

Dad opened the door. It was a small closet, and on the floor was a man tied up in ropes, with a gag in his mouth.

Dad knelt down and quickly removed the gag.

"You!" the man said angrily to Dad. "I might have known. Untie me at once!"

It was the porter from yesterday, thought Molly. George had said his name was Harold.

"What happened?" Adam asked him as he tried to pick at the knots. They were very tight, but Adam knew all about knots from the Secret-Agents-R-Us website and he was pretty sure he knew how to undo these. They were very old-fashioned knots—the kind people used to use centuries ago.

"It was some skinny old geezer with white hair and big eyebrows and a bandage on his forehead," the porter said.

George, thought Molly.

"He and a nasty-looking woman in an old-fashioned maid's uniform."

Lucinda. Lucinda and George, together. Then George must be on her side. Then George must be . . .

George was a ghost. George must have gotten rid of the real porter. He'd tricked her and Adam and even their dad into trusting him, and then he had gone and locked them up here in the dungeon. It was all a plan—Lucinda's plan, obviously. That was why she'd sent Henry to delay them, so she'd have time to switch the porters. No wonder Molly had felt everything was happening too easily.

And that business about that helmet. Could it have been George's own helmet? Could he have been the one shot in the head centuries ago and still angry about the injustice of it? Still hanging around his own helmet as a ghost and hoping for revenge? She wondered how he knew so much about the collection and the college. And then she realized it had to be all those years of haunting it—he must have heard porters and wardens over the years and become as knowledgeable as anyone.

But if he was a ghost, then how could he have opened the door and locked it? How could he hold the keys? How could he shake her dad's hand?

There was just one way. Lucinda had told him how to get his body back. Told him so she could use him to get them locked up.

She was adding more soldiers to her army of angry dead people—and George, clearly, was one of them.

Molly's thinking was interrupted by a laugh. By *the* laugh. The laugh that always sent chills down Molly's spine.

CHAPTER EIGHTEEN

A Haunting Party

It was Lucinda, of course. Molly looked around. Lucinda was here, somewhere. Was she ever going to get tired of using that lame laugh to try to scare people? Apparently not. Molly grimaced as Lucinda appeared, cackling away. Seeing Lucinda pop in out of nowhere, the real porter fainted, still bound in the ropes, although it looked like Adam was making some headway.

And where was Granddad? Wasn't he supposed to have kept Lucinda away? And if he couldn't do that, wasn't he supposed to have warned them? What had happened?

"Lucinda," said Dad with a sigh.

"It's me, all right," she said with a nasty grin. She pointed at the elephant, which Dad was still holding. "I'll take that."

"I don't think so," Dad said.

Her eyes narrowed and her smile disappeared as she glared at him. "We'll see about that," she said. Then she turned her eyes up toward the curved ceiling. "Gentlemen!" she called. "Your services are required."

And so quickly that it made Molly blink, there were three more people standing behind Lucinda. All three were brandishing swords.

"You lot have no respect for we servants and poor folk," said George, one of the three who had appeared. "Typical monarchists."

There was no longer a bandage on his forehead, and blood was pouring down his face. If he was bleeding that much, Molly realized, he had to be back in his body again.

"If these are thine enemies, sweet damsel in distress," said the second to Lucinda with a low swoop of his weapon, "then I shall chop them off at the knees." It was the knight from yesterday—Sir Eustace.

"We wish that ill-favoured geegaw," said the third to Molly's dad, looking over at the elephant. "And We wish it now, varlets!" It was Henry the Eighth.

"Who dares defy the wishes of the monarch?" he said.

"Not I, Your Majesty" said Sir Eustace with a bow of his head.

"Nor I, Sire," said George, with a bow from the waist. "Although I don't usually bow to monarchs, I respect you for her sake." He pointed to Lucinda.

"As you should," said Henry. "Give the geegaw to the lady. Now!"

"We'll die first!" Molly shouted, stepping in front of her dad. It sounded very melodramatic and over the top, but somehow, when you were surrounded by knights and kings with apparently very sharp swords, it seemed appropriate.

And besides, at least some of them were ghosts. Maybe.

With a huge gulp of air, Adam joined Molly in front of his dad. It was his nightmare come true and worse. The terrifying knight, Sir Eustace, apparently hadn't believed what they told him about Lucinda and was back on her side, and he was accompanied by a couple of even angrier fellows. But the entire world was at stake, after all. Not to mention his dad. What choice did he have?

And anyway, at least some of them were still ghosts. Maybe.

"You dare refuse Us?" the king bellowed. When he did, Molly finally understood what the word "bellowed" really meant. The whole room shook. "You dare defy Us, the king? We have cut off heads for less!"

"Well," said Dad, surprisingly calm as he pushed Molly and Adam aside and stepped between them, "I'm sure you have, Sir. But we're not in your time anymore, are we? Now we have laws and rules, and you would be nothing more than a common criminal if you hurt me. The police would put you in jail."

"No one can put Us in jail," he shouted. "We are the law!"

"Maybe you were," said Dad, "once, a long time ago. But this is the twenty-first century. Think before you act, Sir. Do you want to come back into your body only to spend the rest of your life locked up? In fact," he added, "the police are on their way here right now."

Dad was bluffing, of course.

Lucinda saw through it. "You can't hold us," she taunted him.

"Certainly not," said Henry scornfully.

"You or your police or anyone," Lucinda added. "If the police do appear—which I very much doubt they will—and they lock us up, we could escape whenever we wanted, so do as he tells you, and hand over the elephant, because I can assure you that those swords are all real."

But, Molly wondered, were they really? The knight and the porter were one thing, but the king was a different matter altogether. He was very pushy and very obstinate. Lucinda was certainly clever enough to know she'd have to think hard indeed before telling him, of all people, the secret of getting his body back.

And come to think of it, the same went for Sir Eustace. He was a big, burly fellow, and if he wanted to, he could easily overpower someone like Lucinda. And he got angry fast. He might want control, at some time or other. She'd be taking a gamble with him, too.

George was another matter. They knew for sure that he had his body back. He'd managed to use the actual keys to lock the door and open up the case. But again, Lucinda was no dummy—if she'd given him his body back, it had to be because she knew she could trust him. But how could she know that?

Molly gave George a careful look—and noticed something strange: He wasn't bleeding anymore. He looked exactly the same otherwise, but the blood was no longer dripping down his forehead. Which meant . . .

Which meant he was dead again, and out of his real body. It was perfectly logical, too: that was a serious wound he had there. It had killed him in the first place, and once he was back in his body, it would very quickly kill him again. As it must have done already now, without George or the others even realizing it.

And come to think of it, Henry had asked them to hand the elephant over to Lucinda—not to himself. Could that mean he was incapable of holding it? Still a ghost? It seemed logical.

Well, Molly told herself, the only way to test a theory was to try it out. What did she have to lose?

Only a few gallons of blood.

On the other hand, there was the world. And Dad. And Adam. They all needed to be saved.

Molly took a few steps closer to the king, reached out her hand and touched the hilt of his sword. Her hand went right through. So far, so good. Taking another very short step forward, Molly reached out and touched Henry's arm. Her hand went through that, too.

So he wasn't solid like Lucinda.

Well, Molly thought, it's now or never. She rushed behind Henry and, reaching out both hands, thrust them toward Sir Eustace and George. Toward—and through!

"Hah!" she exclaimed.

Henry turned and slashed his sword at Molly. It went right through her, as did the other two.

"And hah again!" she said. "I knew you were still ghosts!"

"Good work, Molly!" said Dad.

But then, with a sudden blow of her fist, Lucinda smashed through the glass on top of a nearby display case. She reached into the case and brought out a gleaming silver dagger.

"Now I suggest you give that elephant to me," she said as she turned and grabbed Adam with one arm. With the other she held the point of the dagger against the side of Adam's neck. Her voice was low and steely and somehow much scarier than Henry's bellowing.

"Don't move an inch or I'll slit your throat," she told Adam. "And don't think I won't—by now you ought to know me better than that. And you, girl," she said to Molly, "you come over here and stand by me, too."

"No, don't, Molly!" her dad shouted at her, but

Molly was not going to argue with a dagger at Adam's throat.

"And now," Lucinda said, "I have you exactly where I wanted you in the first place. Except you shouldn't have that elephant. I expected to get here well before you could get your hands on it. But I ran into some silly interference. But I'm here now. So give it to me!"

It had been a trap, just as Molly had suspected.

But why? What good was it going to do Lucinda to have them all trapped in a cellar?

And what was going to happen to them now?

CHAPTER NINETEEN
The Haunter's Hostages

"It's very simple," said Lucinda to Dad, "and I am sure you will see the logic of it as soon as I say it. You bring me the two jewels after giving me the elephant, and then I let your brats go free."

Adam did not like the sound of that. He and Molly were hostages. Hostages to a ghost, of all things. Boy, this was just stupid.

"So," Adam said before he could stop himself, "once you have the jewels and all your dead friends come back into their bodies and the world as we know it is destroyed, what difference will it make? We'll all be dead, anyway. Sorry Molly," Adam added. "Not like I'm not worried about you."

"But you're wrong, Adam," Molly said. "We're better off alive, even if we are hostages."

She was right, of course. As long as they were alive,

there was still a chance they could do something. Escape somehow, maybe, or . . .

Or something. But better to keep on being hostages than just giving up.

"If you think I'm leaving my daughter here with you," Dad told Lucinda, "you're crazy. I don't care, I'm not budging."

Lucinda laughed and said, "Fine. Send the boy, then, and you wait here with the girl."

Lucinda quickly moved the dagger. Now it was pointing at Molly's neck instead of Adam's.

Adam was more than a little taken aback by this new idea, but he could see how smart Lucinda was being. Adam would do anything to save his dad and his sister—including bringing Lucinda the jewels.

"What's this?" A groggy voice interrupted. "Where am I? Wha—?"

It was the porter, who had finally regained consciousness.

"Silence, knave!" Henry shouted. He strode over to where the porter lay on the ground near the door to the closet and tried to kick him. His foot went right through the porter's arm, which made Henry so angry he slashed at him with his sword, which, of course, went right through him, too. Henry roared.

The porter stared up at him with wide eyes, and then said, "I'm imagining things, obviously. None of this is happening."

Lucinda laughed.

"But," the porter continued, "imaginary or not, I'm not putting up with any silly nonsense. This is college property, and you have no right being here."

Lucinda laughed again. Henry kicked the porter again. His foot went through the porter again. Henry roared again.

The porter was more awake now, and very angry. "I know who you are," he said to Lucinda. "You and that white-haired geezer"—he tilted his head toward George—"you're the ones who tied me up like this and locked me in the closet. You'll be laughing out of the other side of your mouth, my good woman," he said, "when I call the police! And," he was looking around at all the others now, "what is this? Some kind of fancy dress party? Some secret-society initiation, maybe? We had one of those back a few years ago, a bunch of lazy undergraduates it was, and they left burn marks and cigarette butts and empty beer cans all through the crypt. I'm not having it, I tell you. Untie me, now!"

"Actually," said Lucinda, "that's not a bad idea. Untie him, George."

George was bleeding again, Adam noticed—he must have noticed he was ghostly again and then done whatever it was the ghosts did to get back into their real bodies. George nodded and began to work on the ropes.

"Notice, however, where this dagger is located," Lucinda told the porter, holding it right up against Molly's neck. "One wrong move and the girl will pay. I don't mind killing her. In fact, I've been rather looking forward to it. Understand?"

The porter glared at her angrily and then nodded.

"Good," she said. "Here's what's going to happen. You will accompany this boy to wherever he needs to go to get those jewels. You can take him there in one of those automobile contraptions, perhaps. And you can confirm his story in case anyone decides not to take the word of a mere child."

Mere child, eh? Hah! Well, Adam, thought, it's probably a good thing Lucinda was underestimating him. It might actually give him a chance to do something. And hey, maybe it'd be a good idea to make sure she kept on thinking how "mere" he was.

"I'm not a mere child," he said, in the whiniest voice he could muster. "I'm not! I'm not! I'm not! I'm almost all grown up now. I am!"

Dad stared at him as if he were crazy. But Molly immediately understood what he was doing, and gave him a small wink—a very small one, so as not to move her head any closer to the point of the dagger.

"Yes," said Lucinda with a sour look, "the little baby clearly needs some adult supervision."

By now, George had undone all the ropes, and the porter was beginning, very slowly, to climb to his feet.

Once up, he wavered a little, looking much the worse for wear. The blood that had dripped on him from George's wounds while George was untying the knots hadn't helped any.

"Now"—Lucinda turned to Adam—"go and get those jewels."

"Now!" Henry yelled. "Move, boy! Move! We want those jewels and We want them now!"

"It's the only thing to do, Adam," said Dad. "I'll stay with Molly. You go find the jewels."

"I will," said Adam, who suddenly had an idea. "But first, before you send me away from my dear, dear sister and my daddy, may I, please, please, pretty please, may I give them a parting hug?"

Lucinda looked at Adam as if he were completely deranged.

"Please, please, please?" he pleaded. "It may be the last time I ever see them—or they ever see me. I'll miss my daddy ever, ever so much, Ma'am."

"I suppose." Lucinda sighed impatiently. "But make it quick."

Adam rushed over to his father and put his arms up. As his father returned the hug, Adam whispered to him. "Quick, Dad, the phone!"

"Right," Dad whispered. Hugging Adam with one arm, he used his other hand to stick the cell into the pocket of Adam's jeans.

"Farewell, my lad," he said dramatically as he did it.

There was no point in Adam taking a chance on saying anything to Molly—Lucinda was still standing right there beside her, gripping Molly's arm and holding the point of the dagger to her neck—so he gave her a quick wave and what he hoped was an encouraging look.

For a brief moment, Adam thought of claiming that they didn't know where the jewels were. But it wouldn't work. Lucinda had obviously overheard his dad and knew they had found the pendant. Stalling would get him nowhere.

With a last look at Molly, he walked over to Harold, the porter. "Come on," he said. "We need to get out of here."

And maybe, Adam thought, call the cops.

But no, that wouldn't do any good either. After all, what could they do? It was like Lucinda said—pointless. The police couldn't shoot a ghost. Although maybe they could wrestle the dagger from her. But could they do that before she sliced Molly's throat? And then Lucinda would just disappear, and pop up again somewhere else to do yet more damage.

Adam needed help. He needed Reggie and Mom and hopefully Granddad. Where was Granddad, anyway? Why hadn't he been here to warn them? Why wasn't he here to help them now?

But it was Mom he had to try to call first. She had her phone with her, too.

Adam took the porter by the sleeve and pulled him out the door. As they began to head up the stairs, he could see George shutting it behind them.

The minute they were up the stairs and out into the cloisters Adam called his mom. He listened, desperate, as her phone rang and rang, but she didn't answer. Reluctantly, Adam gave up. He felt completely defeated. What could he do now?

"Lend me that phone of yours, boy," said the porter. "I'm calling the Old Bill, right now."

"The Old Bill?"

"The coppers," said the porter impatiently, "the police."

"Oh, no," said Adam. "I don't think that's a good idea."

The porter gave him a piercing look. "Now see here, laddie," he said. "Not only has them villains down there tied me up and broken into the college, but they're holding that little lass hostage, right? And your father!"

"Yes," said Adam, "but it's too dangerous. Molly and Dad might . . ."

"Look, lad," said the porter sympathetically. "This is obviously no secret-society initiation, right? Them people are serious, right?"

"Right," said Adam.

"Tell me what's going on, lad. Maybe I can help."

This little old man help against Lucinda and her

powerful ghostly forces? Adam almost laughed. "Do you really want the truth?" he asked.

"I do."

So Adam told him the short version. Even at that, it took quite a while.

"So you see," he concluded, "that bunch down there with my dad and my sister are ghosts. The police can't help. Don't you think I'd want the police if I thought it would do any good?"

The porter looked at him for a long minute. "Suppose what you tell me is true," he allowed, "although honestly, I still think it's the most far-fetched prank I've heard. But say it is true—the police can still help. They are hostage negotiators. Ghostly or real, they know their business."

Adam had to agree. Even so, he pushed the redial on the phone. Still no answer. Where could they all be? What was happening?

"So you go and get these jewels they want," said the porter, "and I'll tell the police what you have told me. And they can judge what best to do. That's all I can promise," he added. "After all, that dagger is real."

Adam nodded. It was all too real, all too sharp.

"And should anything happen to that girl on my watch because I didn't call the Old Bill, well, I'd never be able to live with myself."

Adam didn't have time to argue. From what he knew, even if the police did get here, they wouldn't do anything like break down the door—well, they couldn't with that door anyway—but they would certainly try to talk to Lucinda and Henry and the others. They would conclude that they were all crazy, probably, and go slow so as not to spook them—so to speak. And hopefully that would give Adam enough time to figure out a plan. And Mom and Reggie, too, if he could get hold of them. And Granddad, if he could get hold of him.

But he couldn't reach any of them—and so he had to get to Toot Baldon, somehow, and find out what was going on. The police seemed to be the only possible answer. With a sigh, he handed the cell over to the porter.

CHAPTER TWENTY
The Old Bill Joins the Hunt

It seemed like an eternity before the police actually showed up—two of them, a man and woman, both in the black-and-white uniforms and those funny checkered hats that police in England wear. To Adam, they looked more like bus drivers than cops. And no guns, not like at home.

But after they grilled Adam and the porter about what was happening, and after they heard about Molly and Dad being hostages, it took no time at all for the man to call in for backup and then head downstairs, while the woman ushered Adam out to their car. Adam was relieved that he and the porter had managed to get the police into action without once mentioning ghosts.

The police car was parked right outside the college gates, and right beside some of those double yellow lines that meant "No parking by anybody ever. Except the police."

As they drove, Adam kept punching the redial button on the phone, and the police officer kept asking Adam for more details.

"And the hostages—you know them?"

"It's my sister and my dad!" Adam exclaimed.

"And you think this woman will release them if she gets these jewels?"

For a while Adam didn't answer. It was a very good question. Could Lucinda be trusted?

"Probably not," he finally said in a gloomy voice.

"Don't worry about it too much," she said sympathetically. "These hostage situations usually end up better than anyone ever thinks they will."

"And if she does get the jewels," Adam said, thinking aloud, "then . . . ?"

"That probably won't happen either," the officer said. "We'll just get the jewels and let her take a look— use them to negotiate. We won't actually give them to her. We don't do that, ever."

Yeah, sure, thought Adam. This police officer obviously had no idea about who she was up against, or what might soon be happening to the world and everyone in it.

And—a horrible new thought had occurred to him—how were they ever going to keep any of this a secret? Soon, for sure, the media would show up at the college, and cameras and TV and everyone would find out that ghosts are real and the whole world would freak out.

He tried not to think about the danger that Molly and his dad were in. After all, the police officer was right about one thing; they had a pretty big bargaining chip in the jewels, and between Adam and Mom and Reggie and Granddad, maybe they could figure out a way to end it all.

The officer was still rambling on, doing her best to reassure him. Her cheerful optimism was kind of comforting, even if she knew nothing about the real truth or how serious the situation was.

She did, however, know how to drive fast. In no time at all, they were out of the city and careening down the road toward Toot Baldon.

"My name is Constable Conolly," she said, "but you can call me Sandy. Everybody does. I'm sure there's nothing to worry about, young man. Your family will soon be safe and it'll all be——!"

She shrieked as she gave the steering wheel a sharp turn and almost ran the car right into a tall hedge on the side of the road. With a quick save, she turned back onto the road and stepped on the brakes. The car screeched to a halt.

What was happening? Nothing, as far as Adam could see. But now Sandy was leaping out of the car and throwing open the back door.

"You, Sir," she shouted, "are under arrest."

Adam swivelled his head around.

Of course. He should have known. It was Granddad!

"Sneaking into a police car is against the law, sir— or at least it ought to be. You nearly scared me out of my boots." She began to reach toward Granddad to pull him out of the car.

"It's okay," Adam screamed. "He's my Granddad!"

"Your Granddad?"

Adam nodded.

Sandy turned back to Granddad. "How on Earth did you get in here?" she demanded. And she looked pretty stern when she said it. She might be quite pretty, with blonde hair and blue eyes and a small frame, but Adam suddenly thought he wouldn't like to get on her wrong side.

"I'm terribly sorry, my dear," said Granddad gently. "I didn't mean to startle you. It was quite thoughtless of me."

Thoughtless indeed, thought Adam. It had almost forced him and Sandy over onto the astral plane with Granddad and the rest.

"But," Granddad went on, "if you're going to help us, young lady, then I think you'd best know the truth." And with that he disappeared.

Sandy stared at the spot where he'd been sitting.

"How did he do that?" she asked Adam, who was

still in the car.

A moment later, Granddad was back.

"Stop that!" she demanded.

Granddad floated out of the car and stood beside her.

"Put your hand on my shoulder," he said.

She did. And it went through him.

"You see, my dear," said Granddad, "I'm a ghost. I *am* his grandfather, but I'm afraid I'm dead. Have been for some decades now, in fact. That woman who is holding my granddaughter killed me, and she's very dangerous. If you could just drive this lad to my old house in Toot Baldon, then we can develop a plan. I hope."

Adam wondered why Granddad had chosen to reveal his ghostiness just when they needed to hurry. They couldn't afford to waste precious minutes trying to convince someone of something she would never believe.

Sandy ran her hand through Granddad's shoulder again. "How do you do that?" she whispered. Then she added, "I must be cracking up. They said the stress would get to me some day."

Adam got out of the car and went over to her. "Sandy, I'm afraid that this is very real, and we don't have time for you to freak and then wait forever for you to finally accept it. It's like *Doctor Who*, right?" He loved *Doctor Who*, and he'd just remembered it was the favourite show in England. "On *Doctor Who*, at first no one can believe the weird things that happen, but some do right away—the really clever ones. You should be one of those. Then we could just jump in the car and go on with the chase."

This actually seemed to make sense to her. "I see what you are saying," she agreed. "In that case, we'd better get going." She began to climb back into the car.

Adam loved British people. They were so sensible and didn't go hysterical over every little thing like aliens or ghosts. Maybe he'd move here when he grew up. He could go to New College like his dad and Granddad. If there was a world to grow up into.

Adam joined Sandy in the car. Granddad floated himself in through the closed door, and off they went.

"Granddad, where were you?" he asked, trying not to make it sound too accusatory.

"I'm so sorry, Adam," Granddad answered. "I've just been down in the dungeon and found out what's happening there. Lucinda still has Molly by the throat, I'm afraid. I would have warned you all if I could have, but thanks to Lucinda and her cronies, I couldn't. She's one canny lady, I'll give her that—after she figured out how to get out of that time prison we had her in, she quickly figured out how to make one herself. Although, you know, I suspect she had some help from some dis-contented alchemists still pursuing their devilish ex-periments on the astral plane. She rigged one up, at any rate, and managed to catch me and Shorty in it. It was a lot stronger than the one we had her in, too; it took us what felt like forever to figure out how to get out of there. Finally, though, I did get away and found the situation out of control."

"Out of control is right," echoed Adam. And then he added, "I suppose putting you in prison is what delayed her long enough for us to get hold of the elephant before she did, but that didn't really help us anyway," he sighed.

"I'm not sure what we can do to stop her," said Granddad. "I'm very worried. And," he added, "she doesn't just have Henry the Eighth on her side now. She's collected a sizeable army of ghosts, it seems, and most of them are quite nasty; a number of criminals such as John Dillinger, Dick Turpin, Blackbeard the Pirate, and she has Billy the Kid recruiting among the desperadoes of the Wild West. I've heard that Napoleon wants in, too—and the Roman emperor Nero. Let's just say that if she gets her hands on those jewels, I doubt that the world can survive. As it is, she's had to use all her strength to hold the ghosts back and keep them in line. And once they come back into their bodies and get their hands on weapons, well, what's to stop them from just blowing up the world in their quest for power?"

"Not to mention the living all dying at the same time," said Adam, remembering the words of the poem.

"Not to mention that," Granddad nodded. "The scariest thing is, I really don't think Lucinda cares."

"Wait a minute," said Sandy as the car roared down the road and into the village. "Are you saying that the fellow who thinks he's King Henry really is King Henry?"

"Yes," said Granddad. "He is, I'm afraid."

"Oh, dear," she said. "That's not good, not good at all."

"And," added Granddad, "how we stop them and save Molly at the same time, I'm not sure."

They pulled up to the cottage then, and Sandy stopped the car.

How, Adam thought, am I going to tell Mom what's happening?

If I can find her, that is.

CHAPTER TWENTY-ONE
Haunting News

A dam ran from the car into the house, with Sandy right behind him and Grandfather floating above them both.

"Mom! Reggie!" Adam shouted.

But there was no answer. In a panic, he raced through all the rooms on the main floor, then rushed up the narrow stairs and looked upstairs.

No one. The house was empty.

Now what, thought Adam? He had been counting on them to figure out what to do next. And he was scared, too—what might Lucinda have done to his mom?

But as he slowly made his way back downstairs, Sandy called him into the kitchen.

"Adam," she said, "look—out there—is that them?"

Adam rushed over to the window that overlooked the back garden. Sure enough, there were some people under the tree where the tree house was—where John had buried the pendant.

Yes! It was Mom! And Reggie. What were they doing out there?

Adam charged out of the house, Sandy behind him.

"Adam," said Mom, as he reached her and threw his arms around her. "What's that for?"

"It's just so good to see you!" he said.

"What are you doing here?" said Reggie. "Where's your father, where's Molly? And who's this?" He motioned toward Sandy.

"Sir," said Sandy, "my name is Constable Sandy Conolly, and I must speak to Mr. Barnett's wife."

Mom, still being hugged by Adam, suddenly tensed. "Adam!" she said as she pulled his arms from around her neck. "What's going on?" In a way, Adam was relieved that Sandy would be the one to break the bad news.

"Lily, dear," said Granddad as he popped into view, "there's been a bit of a worrying development."

"Perhaps you would like to come inside and sit down?" Sandy said.

"No," Mom said, drawing herself up. "What is it? Tell me now."

"There's been an incident at New College," Sandy began.

Mom interrupted. "Where's Molly? Is she all right? Where's your dad, Adam?"

"The thing is," Adam said in a small voice, "Lucinda

218

has them."

"What?" said his Mom, the colour draining from her face. Reggie took her arm and kind of held her up because her knees seemed to buckle.

"I'm afraid it's true," said Sandy. "This woman has taken both your daughter and your husband hostage in the crypt of New College Chapel. The police are there, along with our best hostage negotiator." She paused, looking quite uncertain. "Your son, however, has told me that this is not your ordinary hostage taking and your father—father-in-law?"—Mom nodded at that— "Well, he says he's a ghost."

"I do," said Granddad. "I am."

Mom looked surprised for a moment, but she had no time to worry about why they'd confided in the constable. "He really is," she confirmed. "I'm sorry."

From the look on her face Adam could tell that Sandy had no idea whether she'd just happened upon some kind of weird cult, whether she'd lost her mind, or lastly, whether it was all actually true.

"No apologies necessary," she finally said. "Would you like to accompany us back to the chapel?" she offered. "They seem to want you to bring some jewels to exchange for your family members. Do you know what they're talking about?"

"Yes," said Mom. "But . . . but if we give them these jewels, much worse things will happen than having two hostages."

Now Sandy looked really shocked. His mom seemed more worried about some stupid gems instead of the life of her own husband and children. Adam didn't suppose she'd believed a word about the world ending.

"I think that before we go back, we need a plan," said Granddad. "Let's go into the house, sit down, and think about this for a moment or two."

"Actually," Mom said, "that's a very good idea. Some clear thinking will do us all good."

Adam sighed. She was probably right. But how could she keep so calm, when stuff like this was happening? In fact, he realized, she wasn't calm at all; she was probably frantic inside, but was handling it the best way she knew how—by being in control. That was Mom all over. Thank goodness.

As they headed back for the house, Reggie turned his head and began shouting at the tree they'd just been standing under.

"Sorry, Reggie," he said, "but something's come up—something really important. We'll be back as soon as we can."

Reggie was talking to himself now?

"I understand," said a voice from the tree—Reggie's voice.

But, no, it wasn't quite Reggie's voice. Almost, but not quite. As Adam looked back over his shoulder to see where it was coming from, a figure stepped out from behind the tree.

Ah, yes. Regina, Reggie's ancestress—the one who was looking after little John.

"She's the reason we were out here," said Mom. "Her and the poor little boy."

"Yes," said Reggie. "We were pretending to search the attic when we heard this awful howling out back."

"And when we went to investigate," said Mom, "it turned out to be the little boy."

"John," said Adam. "John Barnett."

"That's right," said Reggie, "that's what Regina told us."

"The little lad was in a terrible state," said Mom. "Once you dug up that pendant, Adam, he was free to go—free to try and find his mother. So Reggie—Regina, I mean, the one from the old days—helped show him the way. And he did actually see his mother, off in the distance."

"But," said Reggie, "as he started to run toward her, he was stopped, somehow."

"He said it was as if the air suddenly turned thick, like glue," Mom added.

"Yes," said Reggie, "and he couldn't move forward. That was the howling we heard—John seeing his mother, but not being able to get to her."

"Poor kid," said Mom.

Adam thought that would be truly awful—seeing someone you love, but not being able to reach them. Just as awful as seeing someone you love with a dagger at her neck.

They reached the house. Mom ushered Sandy into the living room and offered her a seat, then perched on the arm of the sofa. Adam and Reggie dragged in some chairs from the kitchen, and Granddad just sort of hovered in the midst of them all.

"When we got out there," said Reggie to Adam, "Regina was already there, trying to comfort the boy. She says she's really worried about him now. We had a long talk about it with her, your mom and I, and we promised to try to help."

"I'm glad," said Adam, "that poor little kid deserves a break for a change. But why can't he get to his mother?"

"Something is still holding him here, obviously," said Reggie. "Him and Regina. But perhaps your Granddad will be able to help us figure it out, once this other business is over."

Reggie seemed absolutely convinced that this other business would, in fact, be over, and soon. Adam wished he could be so confident.

"Now what's the next step?" asked Mom.

Adam thought feverishly.

Maybe they could just pretend to give Lucinda the jewels—say they were in a plain brown paper bag, maybe—and get Lucinda to hand over Molly before she realized that the bag just had some hard-boiled eggs or something in it.

Except that was really lame. Lucinda would never fall for it. Adam looked around. The room was eerily quiet. Apparently no one else had any good ideas either.

"The door was open," said a voice from behind Adam, "so I just came on in. Hi, everybody!"

As Adam turned to see who it was, Reggie leapt from his chair. "Lennie!" he said as he rushed over to his twin brother. "What brings you here?"

"An airplane!" said Lennie proudly. "I actually got on an airplane! I didn't even take any pills!"

"Amazing," said Reggie, grabbing his brother's hand and giving it a vigorous shake. "But why did you come?"

"I don't know, really," said Lennie. "It was just . . . well . . . I woke up from a nightmare, just as this strange man was about to push me off the edge of this high building. And I had this odd feeling. Like you were in trouble—all of you. Like you needed me here. I just somehow knew I had to come."

"Imagine," said Reggie proudly. "You on an airplane, and flying all the way from Palm Springs!"

So Lucinda hadn't ever really put Reggie's life in danger, thought Adam, she'd just given him very bad dreams. As Adam said hello to Lennie, he remembered Lennie once saying that twins often had a kind of psychic bond and just knew if the other needed help. Well, they certainly did need help now, and fast, too.

Wait a minute! Twins! Yes! Twins!

Adam had suddenly had his own light-bulb moment!

It was obvious they would need to trick Lucinda—he'd already figured that out with that lame idea about the hard-boiled eggs in a brown paper bag. But that wasn't the way to do it. Luckily, Adam had just realized how.

With twins, of course! And with sleight of hand. Adam thought back to all the magic shows he had seen. You make people look one way, and then do something in the other direction that they don't even notice. Why couldn't that work on ghosts, he thought? In fact, it might work better. After all, the ghosts they were dealing with had died a long time ago; they didn't know all the things people know now about how magic works.

"Mom," Adam said. "Do we have any soap?"

His mother looked at him as if he had lost his mind. "Adam, I appreciate staying clean as much as the next mom, but now is not the time to worry about it."

"No, Mom, "Adam said, "I've had an idea! I'm going to sculpt an elephant out of soap."

"Elephant?" she said, confused. "Soap?"

"Yeah!" he said. "We still have that auction listing from Messinger and Messinger, right, with the photos of all of Gram's things?"

She pointed. It was sitting right on the table.

"Good," he said. "Now we just need to find two gems that look sort of the same as the ones we have, and along with a fake elephant and two Reggies, I think we can trick them into thinking that we've given them the jewels and that they have the real elephant—and still get Molly and Dad back!"

Mom looked at him with admiration.

"Good for you, Adam," she said. "What's the plan, exactly?"

"I'm not sure yet," Adam admitted after a moment's pause. "But we'll figure out something."

"I'll get the soap, and while you carve," said his mom, "the rest of us will put on our thinking caps and come up with something—I promise. Hmm," she continued, "we need two stones. A green one and a blue one. I know—I have this blue topaz that Tim gave me for my birthday." She held out her hand to show the ring on it.

"Topaz!" exclaimed Sandy. "What a coincidence! I have a green topaz!" She held up her hand to show her own ring. "I do hate to part with it," she said. "My fiancé gave it to me on our first anniversary of being together." She paused. "On the other hand, if it'll save the world . . ."

She took it off her finger.

Mom took hers off too, and Reggie and Lennie got to work prying the stones out of their settings. Mom found the soap for Adam and placed the auction papers in front of him. He settled in at the pine table beside Reggie and began to carve. The soap was a perfect off-white colour, and Adam hoped it would be close enough to fool the ghosts—if only for the moment they would need.

Unfortunately, it did smell an awful lot like roses, but with any luck, Lucinda wouldn't notice that in all the excitement. He was very happy for all the time he'd spent carving clay and soap and anything else he could get his hands on. Molly had always told him it was a waste of time. He'd said art was never a waste of time. She'd said that he was hardly a great artist like— whoever they were. And he'd told her that not every- one could be a great artist but that it was still fun and he liked it. Who knew it would actually be useful!

As Adam consulted the photo and carved away at the soap, Sandy's walkie-talkie went off.

Adam heard a voice, but couldn't quite make out what it was saying.

"Yes, Sir," he heard Sandy say. "As soon as possible."

She looked at them. "This Lucinda has sent a mes- sage out—my guv'ner sounded pretty freaked. He said this voice came out of nowhere. And it told them to get the jewels there or the dad would be the first to die. And they mean soon. As in the next thirty minutes!"

"Time is of the essence, then!" said a voice from the doorway behind Adam. He turned to see who it was.

"Anne Boleyn!" he said aloud.

226

That drew quite a gasp from the others. Mom made a sort of curtsey and so did Sandy.

"Welcome," said Granddad. "We can certainly use your help."

CHAPTER TWENTY-TWO
Hunting Plots and Plans

"I'm afraid I've been in a dreadful prison, which brought back some very bad memories, I must say," Anne said. "It was even gloomier than the Tower and it took me far too long to escape! It gave Henry a lot of satisfaction to see me locked up again, I can tell you— much too much. He shall pay for it, just wait and see if he shall!" She looked down at her skirt. "Dear me," she said. "It was very dusty in there—surprisingly dusty for such a little prison. Hadn't seen a broom in centuries, I wager. My hair must be a mess." She reached up with both hands and removed her head, then held it up in front of the empty space where it had just been.

Surely, thought Adam, she couldn't actually be seeing it?

But she was. "I do look a mess," said the mouth she was holding up in front of her. "Do I not? But still, here

I am, ready to help." She turned the head around and plopped it firmly back on top of her neck. "He will not win this time."

Anne's determination was clear. Adam was very happy to have her on their side. He'd take Anne over that blowhard Henry any day.

Just then he heard a big thump. It was Lennie, who had keeled over. Adam should have realized that he was more likely to react than Sandy. Lennie was very sensitive, and although he was well aware of ghosts and had met them, seeing Anne take her head off really wasn't for the faint of heart. Reggie ran to get him a glass of water. Meanwhile, Granddad told Anne about the latest developments.

"I see," she said. "A clever ruse." She floated over to Adam. "I used to be quite good with my hands. Let me help with the carving." Soon she was hovering over Adam's head, pointing out little details in the picture of the elephant and describing how he could hollow out the indentations so the jewels would fit.

"The problem is," Granddad said, "that we need to get the real elephant away from Lucinda long enough to put the real jewels in its eyes. Once we've done that Lucinda will go back to being a ghost with no special powers at all. Even the things she was doing when we first ran into her—like possessing still-living people— were probably the result of the curse and the fact that the jewels had been taken from the elephant's eyes.

Once the eyes are restored, Lucinda will return to the kind of ghost that can howl and moan and wander about scaring people now and then, but she won't be capable of doing anything else, except maybe knocking over an occasional picture or something." He paused. "So how do we get the real elephant for long enough to put in the eyes?"

"We'll need a distraction," Anne said calmly. "And I believe I can give you that."

"How?" Granddad asked.

"You see, Lucinda isn't the only one who has amassed an army on the other side."

"I know," he said. "I myself—"

"I'm not talking about any paltry desert rats," she said scornfully. "I'm talking about quality. Noble lineage. Blood."

Whatever she was, Adam thought, Anne certainly wasn't a person who believed in democracy and equal rights and all that.

"Before that logger-headed land-fish of a king trapped me," she continued, "I was gathering people as well. Quality people, as I said. I have a sizeable number of monarchs and noblemen who had their heads chopped off or who died in the Tower, including those two precious little princes—they may be small, but they're feisty. I also have many who died before their dreams were fulfilled and are still waiting for a chance to redeem themselves, especially actors and writers, and the younger sons of younger sons who toiled for fame, but died in obscurity. And I have gentlewomen who went unnoticed—only of the best class, of course—and knightly soldiers who died fighting but were never given so much as a medal or even a burial place."

Adam found himself thinking about George, the soldier who'd fought for the rebel Cromwell centuries ago against the king, and who'd pretended to be a porter at New College. And Sir Eustace, of course. Anne certainly didn't have them on her side. Lucinda had probably gotten to them first.

"I have so many," said Anne proudly, "we could never fit them in that room—but I can fill up the room with a snap of my fingers until there isn't a spot not filled with ghosts who would like a chance to do something great before they move on, something to make up for their woes and let them pass. This can be their chance."

Ghosts who wanted to move on—not ones who wanted to get their bodies back and make things tough for living people. Anne was clever, thought Adam, no question about it. She had chosen very carefully; she could save the world and the ghosts at the same time. How cool was that?

"Excellent," said Granddad. "But then one of us needs to be ready to grab the elephant. Now, from what I can gather, when you left Timmie hadn't yet handed it over, but I think we can assume that by the time we get there Lucinda will be holding it? I doubt she'd leave it in Timmie's hands and if she has, well, this plan will be even easier. So, once we have the elephant, we need someone ready to put the eyes in."

"I should grab the elephant," Reggie said. "I'm the fastest."

"And I will be there to give Lucinda the other elephant," said Lennie, who was now sitting up and looking much better. "She won't even notice the real one is gone. Reggie and I can change places really fast—we used to do it back when we were boys to trick our teachers, and it worked every time."

"I have another idea!" Adam piped up. "Maybe we could ask Regina if she'd show up, too! Then Lucinda would see three of you all at the same time! She'd be confused—just long enough for Lennie to make the substitution."

"Oh, please, may I?" It was Regina, hovering in the air beside Lennie. Lennie flinched.

"It's okay, Len," said Reggie. "She's on our side."

"I do so want to help," said Regina. "I've tried everything to stop that poor lad from being so sad—I even took him up into that old tree house he was so desperate to see, and he pretended to play with the toys for a while. As a nurse, I'm quite pleased that he couldn't pick them up. They're rather filthy, actually—must have been sitting up there for years and years. But well, what harm can it do the lad now? He especially liked the fat little hobby-horse—he wanted ever so much to pick it up, poor boy, but of course he could only look at it. In the end, it only seemed to make things worse. I'd do anything to help him, anything."

"A little hobby horse," Granddad said. "I'd forgotten about that. I wonder . . ."

"But where are my manners," Reggie interrupted. "Lennie, this is our ancestress Regina."

"Uh, delighted, I'm sure," said Lennie, nodding at Regina.

"I think," said Granddad, suddenly recovering from the strange reverie he'd fallen into, "that Adam is the one who should put in the eyes. He can crouch down low, and while all of Anne's friends are screaming and yelling, Lucinda and her crew won't see him do it."

"I'll give you the elephant then, Adam," said Reggie, "as soon as I have it."

"And I'll grab Molly away from Henry or Lucinda or whoever has her," said Mom.

Adam wouldn't like to be either of them—no one was fiercer than Mom if one of her kids was in trouble.

"And I'll help with Anne's ghosts," Granddad said. "I'll get Shorty and the skeleton, too. Begging your pardon, Milady," he added to the queen, "but they really are useful in a crisis. We'll create a kind of organized pageant to make it as loud and as chaotic as possible."

"I suppose a skeleton would be useful in such circumstances," Anne agreed.

Adam put the finishing touches on the elephant, and held it up for inspection.

"How does it look?" he asked.

"Excellent!" said his mom.

"Yes," said Anne with an appraising eye. "Really not bad at all, young sire. You have a gift."

As Adam blushed, Mom turned to Sandy. "Shall we go?"

"Just a minute," Sandy said, "there's something not quite . . . aha! I know! You're going to need someone to offer her the jewels in the first place. After all, that's what she's after."

"That's true," Mom said. "We'd completely forgotten about that."

"I'll do it," Sandy said firmly. "It'll be more believable coming from a copper."

"Well done," said Granddad. "Let's not delay further. I'll go fetch the lads, and then there's something else I have to do, too. Nothing huge, really, but you never know. I'll be there soon." He blinked out.

Sandy took the jewels and put them in her jacket pocket. Then they all piled into the police car and began, so Adam thought, the most fateful journey of their lives.

CHAPTER TWENTY-THREE
THE Return of the Haunted Crypt

"Look," said Dad to Lucinda. "There's no point holding that dagger to my daughter's neck. I mean, you must be getting tired. Your arm must be killing you."

Molly wondered whether using the term "killing" was such a good idea. She had been standing with the dagger to her throat for what seemed like forever. And she knew that Lucinda would just love to kill another Barnett, so she felt like any moment could be her last. Still, she was pretty sure that Granddad and Mom, and of course Adam and his wonderfully warped imagination, would come up with a good plan. So she decided to stay calm. What good would freaking out do anyway?

She was, however, finding it harder and harder to stay in one spot and one position without moving, and she was beginning to fear that a random twitch could get her throat cut. So she was glad her dad was trying to get her away from Lucinda.

"I have something you want," said her dad, holding up the elephant, "and you have something I want—my daughter. Why don't we make a trade? We're locked in here, after all, so you'll still have control even if you do hand her over to me."

Dad was right. Lucinda did want the elephant, but she wanted it only so she could destroy it and forever keep the eyes from returning to their rightful place. It would be folly to give it to her, surely?

Adam had a theory about that, of course—Adam had a theory about everything. And he might be right this time. Maybe Lucinda didn't actually want to destroy the elephant. In case she "died" too.

On the other hand, maybe Adam was wrong.

"Dad," whispered Molly, "don't give her the elephant."

But the whisper wasn't low enough. Lucinda heard it—and it was enough for her. If Molly thought turning over the elephant was a bad idea, then Lucinda was all for it. "Come over here," she ordered Dad.

He did.

"Hand that thing to me while I give you the girl," Lucinda instructed.

Dad slowly offered the elephant and Lucinda lifted the dagger so she could reach for it. As she grasped the elephant in one hand, Dad reached out toward Molly. But then suddenly, he was pushed away.

It was George—bleeding again and real enough to give Dad a big push just at the right moment.

Or, more exactly, the wrong moment. Lucinda grinned. Now she had both Molly and the elephant.

"Good work!" she said to George. "You'll be rewarded for that, my boy."

George smiled proudly. "No need, my lady," he said. "The only reward I expect is the downfall of the evil monarchy! On with the revolution! Let freedom rule!"

Weird, thought Molly. George hated kings so much. Why hadn't he noticed that the other people fighting with him on Lucinda's side included an obedient knight and a very bossy king? Maybe it was all the blood dripping past his eyes that made it hard for him to see things clearly.

Henry and Sir Eustace noticed it, though. Molly could see both of them darting angry looks at George.

Well, at least the dagger was no longer at Molly's throat. It was at her back. Unfortunately, Dad had been pushed all the way behind one of the large display cases. From the dark shadows, he mouthed the word "sorry" to Molly.

She mouthed back, "It's okay." It was, really. No harm had been done—had it?

Lucinda held up the elephant and gazed at it. "Imagine," she said, "this little beauty is mine, now! All mine!

And soon the two stones will join it and my rule will be total." She laughed her horrible laugh.

"Your rule?" Henry bellowed. "We don't think so, maid!"

"Mind your manners, varlet!" said the knight, turning on Henry.

"Who are you calling varlet, knave?" said George. Now all three had their swords up and poised to strike. They stared fiercely at each other.

Molly liked the sound of this. It was always good when the bad guys turned on each other. As she'd seen so many times in movies, it was often their undoing.

"Swords down, my lads," Lucinda said in a firm voice. All three turned, their swords now pointed at her. After a few tense moments of her looking imperiously at them, they did drop their swords—but they didn't look very happy. "Never fear, Your Majesty" Lucinda added meekly. "You shall, of course, rule over all, with me your mere servant."

Molly knew that Lucinda didn't have a meek bone in her body, but she supposed Henry didn't know it.

"Indeed, my liege," Lucinda continued, "I will be your good servant and carry out your orders as we discussed."

"If you believe that," said Molly's dad to Henry, "you'll believe anything."

Henry swivelled toward Dad, furious.

"Mind you," Dad continued, "your judgement was never that great. All those wives, for instance."

Henry glared at him. "What? You dare—?"

"And just look at history," Dad continued in a chatty voice, as if completely unaware of the fury he was creating in the monarch. "Who was arguably the greatest sovereign in all English history? Your own daughter Elizabeth, that's who! And what did you ever do to acknowledge her talents? Just went ahead and got her declared illegitimate, that's all! Shows what you knew. King Henry the Dope!"

Yikes! What, Molly wondered, was Dad doing? Why get Henry mad?

"So," Dad went on, "you might want to reconsider just who you are going to trust."

Now the knight and George had wheeled around and had their swords pointed toward Dad.

"Silence, you crook-pated measle!" said Henry. "This nonentity, this beetle-headed pigeon-egg"—he gestured toward Lucinda—"will have to bow to Us, as will all my subjects," Henry declared, "including you, lout! It is the divine right of kings We rule by, after all!"

Lucinda let out a snicker. She couldn't help herself, thought Molly. If there was one thing Lucinda hated, it was people who thought they were better than her.

Henry rounded on her. "What say you?"

"Oh, nothing," Lucinda said. "Something caught in my throat." She cleared her throat loudly.

"Henry, my friend," Dad continued. "You need to learn something. It's been centuries since people believed in the divine right of kings. Do you really think that all the ghosts who died in the last few hundred years would allow you to rule them? Would Winston Churchill put up with it, for instance? Or Karl Marx, who said that the peasants had nothing to lose but their chains? Or Elvis, or Janis Joplin? No, my chum, the days of divine right are over."

"Winston Churchill?" said Henry. "Who's he? We shall have him hung!"

"That Marx fellow sounds interesting," George piped up.

"He was," said Dad. "Very interesting. And if he's still around—which I suspect he probably is—then I'm sure Lucinda has him lined up behind her. And Elvis, too."

With a flare of fire in his eyes, Henry turned and gazed at Lucinda. "Is this true, barnacle?"

"Why listen to him?" she scoffed. "He'll say anything to get out of here with his dear daughter—and with this elephant. Now is not the time for squabbling. Remember it was me who discovered all of this, who made it all possible. Me! Me! Me!"

Henry looked at her thoughtfully and then turned back to Molly's dad.

"You might be correct, knave," he said slowly.

A loud knock on the door interrupted the discussion.

"We're coming in," said a woman's voice from behind the door. "I'm Constable Conolly, and I have the jewels you've asked for."

"Enter," said Lucinda with a satisfied smirk.

"Before I do," said the voice, "you should know that I've got some people with me. Molly and Tim's family are here, and they insist on seeing that she's safe before we hand over the jewels."

Were they seriously going to just hand over the jewels? Molly thought. Surely not! They must have a plan.

"May we come in?"

Henry opened his mouth to say something. But then he looked at Molly's dad and shut it again. Molly suspected that he had been about to object to having so many people enter the room. As a tactician and warrior he knew that would be a disadvantage to him and to Lucinda's cause.

And yet, he said nothing. Interesting. Molly had to give her dad props. What had seemed to be idle chatter might have given them an advantage.

"Enter!" Lucinda repeated, the thrill of victory evident in her voice.

The door opened.

CHAPTER TWENTY-FOUR

The Haunt of the Hunted Elephant

The first person Molly saw was her mom, and she'd never been so happy to see anybody. After all, if anyone could take on Lucinda, it was her mom. Molly thought about all the times she and Adam had been warned to be careful of bears they met unexpectedly at the lake, especially mother bears protecting their cubs. Well, those bears could learn something from her mom!

Reggie, a policewoman and Adam all followed Mom into the room, and stood clustered together just inside the door.

But no Granddad——was he somewhere else? Had Lucinda imprisoned him again?

"I have the gems," said the policewoman. "This man," she pointed to Reggie, "will walk over to you with me, so that he can protect me should you have a weapon."

Lucinda laughed.

"Show me the jewels," she said. "And walk over here alone!"

"How do I know I can trust you?" said the constable.

You can't, thought Molly glumly.

"You'll just have to take my word for it," said Lucinda.

For a moment the constable hesitated. But then, finally, she nodded her head. "All right," she agreed. "If that's the way it has to be."

Molly mentally crossed her fingers. She sure hoped the constable knew what she was doing.

Lucinda gestured for George to come over. She handed him the dagger so that one of her hands would be free while the other held the elephant. The officer took two small items from her jacket pocket and began to walk toward Lucinda. No one else moved. Molly held her breath.

Then, suddenly, things started happening—happening so fast that Molly couldn't quite make it all out. As the constable moved toward Lucinda, jewels in her outstretched hand, Reggie sprang forward, fast as a cat. And then another figure appeared. It was Anne Boleyn, and she began to shout at Henry the Eighth.

"I will have my revenge, you lob-legged scratch-mouse!" she said in a very loud voice.

As Queen Anne shouted, the constable handed the jewels to Lucinda. She reached out with one hand to take them, and the room suddenly filled with people. Or ghosts. There must have been thirty or forty of them, so many and so twisted around each other that it was hard to make out any individuals. They all began to shout at Lucinda.

"Revenge!" they cried from mouths that opened all over the crypt. "Revenge!"

Lucinda, now holding the jewels in one hand, dropped the elephant from her other.

But no, wait! She hadn't dropped it—Reggie had knocked it out of her hand! And now there was another Reggie, right behind him.

And—was Molly going nuts?—yet another one, also, who suddenly blinked into view right in front of Lucinda, and then blinked out again, and in again, and out again.

Lucinda was looking very confused. As she shook her head to clear it, the Reggie behind Lucinda, who had caught the elephant when Lucinda dropped it, suddenly produced another elephant out of a pocket or somewhere, and shoved it into Lucinda's hand. He moved so fast that he was out of the room in an instant. Now there was only one Reggie. All the other ghosts were gone and Lucinda was left holding an elephant in one hand and the jewels in the other.

As Lucinda stared at the objects in her hands as if she had no idea about what had just happened, Molly felt someone else beside her. It was her mom, who had snuck up behind George while everything else was happening. With a quick move, she grabbed the dagger from George's hand and pulled Molly out of harm's way.

Lucinda didn't care. She didn't even seem to notice. She had what she wanted. She let out a cry of triumph and raised the elephant high. She looked as if she were about to smash it to the ground.

But she didn't. She just held it there, waving it triumphantly in one hand and clutching the jewels in the other. So Adam's theory must have been right, after all. Lucinda wasn't planning to destroy the elephant or the jewels. She was just going to make sure no one else ever got their hands on them. Maybe she'd hand them over to poor Henry or the knight and then ship them off to one of those time prisons. Or maybe she'd just keep them and never let them out of her sight.

One way or another, the world was doomed.

"Doomed!" a chorus of voices chanted. "Doomed! You are doomed!"

All the ghosts who had blinked out just a few moments ago were back, circling Lucinda and chanting, doing silly dances and generally making a big fuss. Among them, Molly could see now, was Anne Boleyn, along with a bunch of people dressed up in old-style hats and coats, some without heads and some with only heads and no bodies. And there was Shorty, too, and the skeleton. And was that Reggie, again, dancing beside the skeleton? Reggie in a dress?

No, of course not! It had to be Reggie's ancestor Regina, and little John was right beside her, dancing happily also.

And there was a very familiar face. Could it be . . . ? Surely it wasn't Gram?

What was happening now?

Adam must know—but where was he? Molly had seen him come in with the others earlier, and then lost track of him. She glanced eagerly around the very crowded and very noisy room. Ah, there he was, crouched over something on the floor near the wall behind one of the display cases.

She raced over to him, passing harmlessly through several dancing and chanting ghosts.

"Adam," she said, "thank goodness you're okay. What's—?"

"I can't do it, Molly," he interrupted, his voice panicky. "I can't get them in! You try!"

He thrust something into her hand. The elephant. And the jewels. But how . . .

Suddenly Molly understood. The jewels and the elephant Lucinda had now were fake! They'd made a switch! These—the ones she was holding in her own hands—were real!

"I can't get the eyes in, Molly," he said desperately, his hand shaking. "We need to get them in! They ought to go in, they have to go in! But they're way too large for the holes!"

"Let me try," she said. Handing Adam the Evening Eye, she desperately tried to push the Morning Eye into the empty socket on the elephant's head.

But Adam was right—it was too large, and the wrong shape. The indentation was a circle, but the gem wasn't round. It was more of a leaf shape, or like an eye.

"Try this," said a voice from behind her. Granddad! He thrust an object toward her.

"Granddad," she said, "you're carrying something! Are you in your real body?"

"Never mind about that, Molly. Take this and try the eyes in it!"

She did as he said, and found herself holding another carving. It wasn't much bigger than the elephant Adam had handed her, and, well, really it was more like a horse than an elephant. But it did sort of have elephant ears—big floppy ones on the sides of its horsy head, and a sort of snout which might be a short elephant trunk.

And holes where eyes might go. Leaf-shaped holes.

Quickly, Molly jabbed the Morning Eye into the hole nearest to her. It fit! And as she did, Adam was doing the same thing with the Evening Eye on the other side! It fit, too! The eyes were finally back where they belonged!

And that's when a gut wrenching sound filled the room. Molly looked to see Lucinda—her mouth wide open, her eyes staring wildly, a scream coming from her throat. It reminded Molly of when the Wicked Witch of the West was being melted by Dorothy in the movie. Lucinda screeched and howled and Molly and Adam leaped up and held the elephant-horse thing between them. The ghosts parted until there was a clear line of sight between the children and Lucinda.

"It's over!" Adam shouted at her. "You will never hurt another Barnett again!"

"Or the rest of the world!" Molly called. "So get lost!" she added.

And Lucinda did, sort of, get lost. As she shrieked, she became thinner and thinner, until they could see through what was left of her. Soon they could hardly see her at all.

"Revenge," she cried in a tiny voice. "Revenge!"

"Fat chance," said Granddad. "I hope," he added.

They had done it! The curse had been broken.

CHAPTER TWENTY-FIVE
Hints of Haunts to Come

"Good work, my loyal subjects," said Queen Anne.

Adam started. He'd expected that all the ghosts would be gone, but Anne was still there, and so were most of the others, and all completely visible.

Visible, perhaps, but surely none of them were in their real bodies any longer? And just because the curse was broken didn't mean that a lot of ghosts weren't still going to be hanging around on the astral plane, just as they always had. The end of the curse, after all, didn't stop ghosts from existing.

Even so, Adam reminded himself, they'd never been so easy to see before the curse. Little John must have been hanging around the garden at The Oaks for years without anyone sighting him, and Sir Eustace must have been here in the crypt for centuries.

But now he could easily see Anne and the rest. Anne had turned toward Henry with a triumphant smile, and now she made a very loud raspberry, right in his face.

"I've been waiting ever so long to do that, milord fat-guts," she said. "And now my work here is done! I have had my revenge, and I have no reason to stay near the mortal field any longer. And those of you"—she turned to the ghosts—"those of you who could not progress until you found some way of making up for your misdeeds—well, you have done so now, my friends and loyal subjects, no question about it. Made up for them in a grand and noble way!"

Many of the ghosts nodded and smiled.

"So," she asked, "who wants to move on with me? Now!"

In an instant, many of the ghosts and Anne were gone, even the one that looked like Gram. That ghost had looked at Molly and smiled and winked, just before she blinked out along with all the rest.

But a surprising number of ghosts were still there—among them Henry; Shorty and Bart the skeleton; Regina and little John; and Sir Eustace and George, who stood with swords in hand over in the corner, eying each other.

And Granddad.

"I wish I could move on," said John, "I wish wish wish it! I want my momma! But I've tried—and I can't."

Molly wondered why he couldn't. They'd found the pendant, after all. What else could be keeping John here with them? It was so frustrating not to know.

"Never mind, laddie," said Regina. "I'm here as long as you need me." At that she pulled a small ghostly doll out of her pocket and handed it to John, who sat himself on the floor to play with it.

"I ought to want to move on," said Granddad. "My dear Dora awaits me, I know she does."

Does she? thought Molly. Had Gram moved on? Should she tell Granddad that she'd seen his beloved Dora, still there on the astral plane? Molly should be able to recognize her own Gram, she thought, but she wasn't sure. It looked like a much younger Gram. She'd read when researching ghosts that they could choose to look the way they wanted. And some chose the way they looked when they were young and healthy, not the way the looked when they died.

But there was really no point in telling Granddad and getting his hopes up.

"I ought to move on," he was saying, "But somehow . . . "

"I know how you feel," said Shorty. "And besides, that gold I found is still out there. If only someone would find the goldarned stuff and get me off the hook."

"And, find my strike too," said Bart the skeleton. The durned fools get close to it—so danged close. And then they just veer off and go away again, dang it!"

"They sure don't make prospectors like they did in the old days," added Shorty. "No gumption, no get-up-and-go! So I guess you and I are stuck here for a while yet, eh, Bart, ol' buddy?"

The skeleton nodded.

Meanwhile, a fight seemed to have broken out on the other side of the room.

"Am not!" said the knight, as he slashed at George with his sword.

"Are, too!" said George, blocking the knight's thrust and making one his own.

"Take it back, you half-witted revolutionary spawn of Satan!" said the knight.

"I won't!" said George. "Monarchs are an anachronism, and useless to boot! It's high time you parasites were removed and the country became a republic."

"Gentlemen!" Granddad shouted. "Please! Can't you take this somewhere else? This is hardly the place for a swordfight!"

"I don't see why not," said the knight. "I died in one on this very spot."

"And my helmet's here!" said George. "But . . . well . . . somehow, I don't feel quite so attached to it anymore."

"Nor I to this place," said the knight. "Which," he said to George, "doesn't mean I don't still think your political views are a load of rubbish."

"Same to you, buster," said George. "Antiquated

bilge, if you ask me. We clearly have a lot to discuss—it might take some time."

"Centuries, even," said the knight. "But, yes, let's take it elsewhere."

"And have a few imaginary pints while we're at it."

They nodded at each other, lowered their swords, and blinked out.

"Ridiculous!" said a loud, pompous voice. It was Henry the Eighth. "With warriors like that, We'd have lost the country to the Spanish years ago." He turned to Lucinda with the kind of look that might actually kill. "So much for your silly plan, you muck-brained harpy," he told her. "We are not even beginning to be amused! We shall return to whence We came and consider more logical ways of regaining our rightful power. Perhaps We might consider explosives!" And with that, he was gone.

"Coward," Lucinda called after him, her body barely visible and her voice barely audible. "Quitter! And you call yourself a king! Hah! Well, you can throw in the towel all you want," she cried defiantly, "but I will never give up! Never!" But her voice was so small that it sounded like a little baby having a tantrum.

"Oh yes you will, Missy," said Shorty, "whether you want to or not." He grabbed her by one arm, and Bart grabbed her by the other—and this time, they didn't go through her. She was way less powerful, no question about it. Lucinda was well and truly caught.

"It's off to time prison for you, Missy," said the skeleton.

"And this one's a real doozy," said Shorty. "Even Houdini couldn't get out of it. I know, because I asked him to try it out, and the poor, dumb sap is still there. You and he together can try to find a way out for the next few thousand years or so."

"And," added Bart, as he and Shorty floated upwards toward and through the roof, Lucinda sputtering angrily in their grasp, "there's no time off for good behaviour. Not that we expect any, of course."

"I think Shorty is right," said Granddad as he watched their feet disappear through the arched ceiling. "That's one strong time prison the boys cooked up. She won't be getting out any time soon."

"But Granddad," said Adam. "This thing"—he glanced down at the strange object he was holding in his hand—"I don't understand."

"You can thank little John for that," said Granddad.

"Me?" said John, looking up from playing with his doll.

"Yes," said Granddad, "you. Back there at The Oaks, while we were making our plans, remember, Regina said something about the poor little lad and a hobby horse. Until then, I'd forgotten all about that thing. It was just something that I took for granted—it was just always there, a dusty old thing up in the tree house, along with a bunch of other stuff we used to play with when I was young. Someone before my time must have put the ugly thing there to get it out of the house—and it just stayed there."

"Yes," said Dad, coming over and taking a look at it. "I remember it now. It's the one we always called Bonkers, right?"

"Right," said Granddad. "I did pass that name on to you, didn't I? But to be honest, until today I never thought of it as anything but a weird ugly horse with big ears—that's why I named it Bonkers when I was little, because it was such a crazy-looking thing! I used to hold it in my hand and pretend to ride it to Crazyland, where everyone acted silly all the time. Bonkers Barnetts, we were! But when I went up there to check it today, well, sure enough—I realized it does sort of look like an elephant."

"A deformed elephant," said Molly with an appraising glance.

"But an elephant nevertheless," said Granddad. "And as I was looking at it, I realized that the holes for the eyes it was missing were exactly the same shape as the two gems!"

"But Granddad," said Adam. "How did you get it here? You couldn't carry it, could you?"

"Well, yes, Adam," said Granddad. "As a matter of

fact I could. I did what I had to do. I knew there was no other way."

"Granddad!" said Molly. "You came back into your body."

"I did," he said. "I had no choice, really, if I wanted to get back here with the elephant in time. Although once I got into that car your dad rented and started driving here as fast as I could, I was thinking that it wouldn't be very long before I was a ghost again. It's been yonks since I've driven a car, you know—and the other drivers didn't seem to appreciate the fact that the destiny of the entire planet was sitting on the front seat beside me. Kept getting in my way, they did. It caused a few little traffic-related incidents, I'm afraid."

"Oh, dear," said Sandy, who had been listening intently to the conversation.

"Oh dear, indeed," said Granddad, turning toward her. "But I'm afraid that's not the worst of it, Sandy. You'll find the car parked right outside the gate, a little the worse for wear—and well, the barrier out there on Holywell is just a little bent." His face was a very deep red.

"I'm sure we can find a way to forgive you," Sandy said "Just this once. But I have to say, this has been quite the experience. I'll go report that the coast is clear—although how I am going to explain the lack of suspects I have no idea. I think you must all prepare for extensive questioning." She smiled at them all. "But I'll do my best to smooth the way for you."

Before going, Sandy retrieved the jewels Lucinda had dropped on the floor when she was dragged away. She pocketed one and handed the other back to Molly's mom.

Then they were alone. There was nobody left in the room but Mom and Dad, Adam and Molly, Granddad, John and Regina, and Lennie and Reggie. Nobody but Barnetts and Crankshafts.

There were hugs all around. Even the ghosts hugged and got hugged. They couldn't feel it, of course—not even Granddad, who along with all the other ghosts, had turned back into an insubstantial ghost again as soon as the eyes were put back into the carving, but they all knew what a hug meant.

"You must be our great-aunt, Regina," said Lennie as he and Reggie hugged her. "Our ancestor Fitzie's sister."

"Yes," she said, "it was my brother Fitzie who got me my job nursing Maurice Barnett before he died."

"Maurice was my great-grandfather," said Granddad as he hugged John, "and little John here must be Maurice's younger son. He would have died before you first came to The Oaks, Regina."

"I thought the boy seemed very familiar," said Regina. "He looks like a miniature version of Maurice and Maude's son Percy."

"John's older brother," Granddad nodded, "and my grandfather."

"Which," said Molly, "makes John my and Adam's, let's see, great-great-great-uncle. Weird."

"Weird," agreed Adam, who was just beginning to calm down and take it all in. It was hard to imagine that the little boy standing near him had been born a whole century before Adam himself.

"Another weird thing," said Molly, "is that Lucinda never even knew she had the wrong elephant."

"Nor did we, Molly," her father said.

For a moment, they all looked at the elephant.

"It certainly is an ugly old thing," said Mom. "No one would ever guess to look at it that it was so important."

"So very, very important," Reggie added.

"What on Earth are we going to do with it now?" Molly asked. "We need to guard it with our lives. How do we keep it safe?"

"I know," said her Dad. "We'll donate it to the British Museum—or even better, to the Ashmolean Museum right here in Oxford. They have lots of priceless artefacts that they guard day and night—and nobody would think of looking for it here."

"First," said Lennie, "you'll have to talk them into actually believing it's valuable."

"That might take some doing," said Molly.

"I don't know," said Granddad. "A little demonstration of some ghostly activity might help. Shorty and Bart are still on the loose, remember—and I wager some of that gang that volunteered to fight on our side are still around, too. After the museum officials take it—which I'm sure they will—we'll ask for ghostly volunteers to guard it around the clock. It'll be something useful to do for those who aren't ready to cross over yet."

"I could do that," said Regina.

"But," said Adam, "aren't you going to look after John?"

"I suppose," said Regina, looking a little confused. "Although somehow . . . ," she looked even more confused. "I don't know," she finally said. "I mean, I do like the lad, naturally. But somehow I just don't feel so compelled to do it anymore."

Reggie turned to Mom. "And as much as I enjoy your company, Lily, I don't feel that urgent need to be there for you. Or you either, Adam and Molly."

"Me, too, actually," said Lennie. "I don't necessarily want to get away from you or anything. I still like you all, a lot. A man couldn't have any better friends. But now you feel just like friends—not like people I'm responsible for."

"That exactly how I feel about little John here," said Regina, rubbing his curls with her hand.

"I bet it's the curse," said Adam. "I mean, because your ancestor Fitzie was responsible for giving the elephant to the Barnett family in the first place, you

Crankshafts all felt compelled to watch out for us Barnetts—that was the curse's effect on you, right?"

"Could be," said Reggie.

"That had to be it," said Granddad. "It's amazing how a simple little gift could have led to so much trouble—and also, kept our families connected to each other for so many years, generation after generation."

"Yes," said Regina. "I remember now being drawn to you, too, Ernest, just before you died, just the way I felt drawn to little John. But that time, I was too late to stop Lucinda."

"I wonder," Molly said, "why Fitzie or his father never showed up? Or our ancestor Maurice? They were the ones who started all this, after all."

"I've been wondering about that myself," said Granddad. "I've never encountered either of them anywhere in my travels on the astral plane."

"Probably too ashamed to show their faces," said Reggie.

"Perhaps," said Granddad.

Reggie turned to his ancestress. "Regina, you'd like to volunteer for guard duty, would you?"

"I do believe I would," she said. "There's still something holding me here, it seems—although I have no idea what it is. Something to do with—" she stopped suddenly, a blush appearing on her cheeks. "Uh, never mind. What about you, little John? Would you like to do guard duty with me?"

"Could I?" he said in an excited voice, as he jumped to his feet. "That would be super!"

"It's agreed, then," she told him. "And maybe we can help each other to figure out what's stopping us from moving on. Now, though, little man, you've had quite a busy day. Let's go off someplace where you can have a little quiet time."

John nodded, and they all said goodbye to him and Regina. Then the two of them blinked out.

Molly looked at Granddad. "What about you?" she said sadly. "Does this mean you're going to go as well? I mean, you have your proof right?" She couldn't bring herself to tell him about Gram. He'd be shattered if she were wrong about that.

Molly was right, thought Adam, his heart sinking. Granddad hadn't been able to pass on because he'd desperately needed to find the proof that ghosts exist. Now a lot of people were going to know that ghosts existed—important people, people who could arrange to get the elephant into a museum and have it guarded at all times. Ghosts had become a lot more visible to a lot of people than they ever had been—and who knows, maybe they'd still be visible now that the curse was done. Granddad had all the proof he needed. There was nothing holding him back any more.

"If you don't mind," Granddad said, "I'd like to hang around a bit longer. I have a feeling—just a sort of small feeling—I might be needed. And Dora has been without me for so long now! I do miss her, of course, ever so much. But she can wait a little bit longer, I think."

He was looking rather embarrassed. Probably because of the real reason he was staying, Molly thought. She knew him well enough by now to know how much he enjoyed being around them and other people and ghosts, and arranging and doing things.

And if that had been Gram, she'd realize that, too. Maybe she was just waiting around and staying out of sight so he could go on having his fun for a while longer.

"You don't mind, do you?" Granddad asked them.

"We don't mind!" said Adam and Molly together.

"Nor do we, right Lily?" said Dad.

"You're always welcome," Mom said.

Adam was very happy that he'd finally have a granddad—even if he wasn't exactly like other kids' granddads. Actually, the fact that his granddad was a ghost was even better! Imagine the help Granddad could give him and Molly on school assignments! Plus he'd never get tired like other kids' grandparents. And they'd never get lost with him around, and well, Adam just didn't want him to go.

Molly was thinking the same thing. Who knew, they might need to save the world again. And how could they do that without Granddad?

Meanwhile, though, something else was bothering Adam.

"I'm hungry," he said.

"What else is new?" said Molly as they left the dungeon and climbed up toward the light.